"That's it. Beautiful, Kerri. Now just turn a little more toward me. Perfect!"

I adjusted my hips, straightened my shoulders, and smiled at the camera. I was aware of the blond woman on the boardwalk who'd been watching since the shoot started.

The shoot was on a beach just outside of Miami, Florida, near Laurel Beach, where I lived with my mom and two sisters. My agency, Sunshine Models, had booked me for this job for the Waterlilies swimsuit catalogue.

Almost a year ago I'd gone to the Sunshine office in South Beach, Miami, with one of my best friends, Jessa. We'd read an article on models and thought it might be fun to try out. We both knew it was hard to break into modeling, so I was totally surprised when Sunshine offered to take me on right away. Since then I'd been modeling in my spare time, doing ads for local stores and catalogue work.

"Okay, we're done," said the photographer.

I started across the sand to the location van, where I'd gotten dressed and had my hair and *makeup done. As I passed the blond woman, she looked at me and smiled. With her white silk blouse and tan pants, she looked like she belonged in an office. I smiled back.*

I went into the van and changed back into my T-shirt and cutoffs. The blond woman was still there when I got out.

"Hi," she said, walking up to me. "I wonder if I could talk to you for a moment." She handed me a business card.

I looked down at the card. It said NANCY LLOYD, FORD MODELS, INC., NEW YORK.

"Ford Models?" I repeated. Ford is the most prestigious modeling agency in the world.

"That's right," she said. She put out her hand. "Hi, I'm Nancy Lloyd."

"Hi," I said, shaking hands. "I'm Kerri Gold."

"Well, Kerri," said Nancy Lloyd, "I'll get to the point. I'm a scout for Ford, and I'm looking for new faces. Are you with a local agency?"

"Yeah," I said. "Sunshine Models."

She nodded. "Have you given any thought to moving up to a bigger agency? From what I see, I think you may be Ford material."

"Oh my gosh!" I said. This was incredible. Models with Ford did ads with big-name de-

signers and had their pictures on the covers of magazines. A move to an agency like Ford could change my whole life! Then I thought of something. "You mean I'd move to New York?"

"That's right," she said. "Ford has a Miami agency, too, but I think your look could do well in New York. The Fords will want to see the work you've done here first. But if they did take you on, you'd stay in an apartment with other girls and your school would be arranged."

"Wow," I said. Moving to New York and being a Ford model sounded so cool. Then I realized that it would mean leaving behind my mom and my two sisters, Andie and Casey. And did I really want to say good-bye to the swim team, the cheerleading squad, and my best friends in the whole world, Jessa and Heather?

In the end, I decided that going to New York wasn't something I could pass up. Sure, I'd miss home, but I might never get a chance like this again. My mom wasn't happy, but we had a heart-to-heart. I told her how much I wanted to do this, and she was behind me all the way.

Finally, everything was set. The Fords had arranged things in New York, and my bags were packed. Jessa and Heather gave me a humongous good-bye party, and I was off!

Who are the next

FORD
SUPERMODELS
OF THE WORLD™?

Enter a world of glamour,
high fashion, and fun with
six aspiring young supermodels:
Paige, Cassandra, Naira, Kerri,
Katerina, and Pia!

FORD
SUPERMODELS
OF THE WORLD™

MAKING WAVES

by B. B. Calhoun
based on a concept by Liz Nickles

RANDOM HOUSE SPRINTER™ BOOKS

Random House 🏠 New York

Created by R. R. Goldsmith

Library of Congress Catalog Card Number: 94-66352
ISBN: 0-679-86367-2

IL: 10 and up

Manufactured in the United States of America
10 9 8 7 6 5 4 3 2 1

CHAPTER 1

"Brrr," I said. I looked at Naira and Paige, two of my housemates. "Aren't you guys cold?"

Paige glanced at Naira and raised her eyebrows. "*Cold?*" she said.

Naira shook her head, and the zillions of little braids she was wearing swung back and forth.

"No way," she said. "Kerri, it's fifty-five degrees out here."

I shivered in my sweatshirt. "Well, it's cold to me," I said, a little grumpily.

And it was true. Fifty-five degrees *was* cold—if you were in Florida. But this was New York, where I'd been living for the past two months. Back in August the weather had been great, but now it was October...and there was a definite nip in the air.

It was Saturday. Naira, Paige, and I had just finished a shoot for an ad for *Watch Out!* sports watches. Now we were on our way to the Cocoa Bean. The Cocoa Bean's a super-cute coffee bar near where we live with our other housemates, Cassandra, Katerina, and Pia. The six of us are all Ford models, and we share an apartment with our chaperon, Mrs. Hill. Pia's the one who discovered the Cocoa Bean. She's from Italy, and she says it's just like a real Italian coffee bar.

"Boy, if you think this is cold, you're in for a pretty big surprise come December," said Naira.

"I know, I know," I said. "Believe me, I've heard all about these crazy winters you Northerners have up here."

Back when I never imagined that I'd be living in New York, my friends and I used to see the reports on TV of the blizzards up north. Jessa, Heather, and I would crack up watching people slip and slide all over the place. Now the idea of ice and snow was starting to seem a lot less funny. Even though New York was exciting, I wasn't looking forward to my first winter here at all.

"Well, New York can't be as bad as what

I'm used to," said Naira. "There's nothing like the wind off Lake Michigan in February."

"Michigan? Why are you talking about Michigan?" I asked. "I thought you were from Chicago, Ni."

"I am," she said.

"Chicago's *on* Lake Michigan," Paige explained.

"It is?" I said. "Then why do they call it Lake Michigan?"

"Because it also touches Michigan," said Naira. She starting drawing pictures in the air. "You see, the lake is here. And Illinois, where Chicago is, is here. Wisconsin's up there..."

"Okay, okay," I said, "I believe you." I've never had a super sense of direction. When I first got to New York I felt so lost I was terrified to even walk around the corner by myself. I'm slowly learning my way around, but I still feel better when I'm with someone else.

"You know, Kerri," said Paige softly, "if you wore something warmer you might not be so cold."

"Really," agreed Naira. "You should have put on a jacket or something." She grinned. "Or don't you Floridians know what those are?"

3

I glanced down at my clothes. I had on black leggings, a big gray T-shirt, and sneakers without socks. Over that I was wearing a threadbare white sweatshirt that said LAUREL BEACH SWIMMING across the front in green.

For the first time, I noticed that both Naira and Paige had on pretty heavy jackets. Paige was wearing a green corduroy baby-doll dress that set off her long, curly red hair. She also had on wool tights and brown lace-up boots. Over the dress was a brown plaid wool blazer with the sleeves rolled up so you could see the flannel lining. By the way the blazer fit I guessed that it probably belonged to her boyfriend, Jordan. Jordan's in college, and he works at the Cocoa Bean part-time. That's where Paige met him.

Naira was wearing her favorite patched and faded jeans with a black turtleneck and black clogs. On top of that was a purple wool baseball jacket with white leather sleeves. And on her mass of long black braids was a floppy black velvet hat with a purple velvet flower at the brim.

"Yeah, I guess you guys are right about the jacket idea," I said with a sigh.

I had a couple of jackets back at the apart-

4

ment, but it just never occurs to me to put one on. Besides, I can't stand wearing a ton of clothes. I like to be able to move around easily. Heavy clothes always feel like they're weighing me down somehow.

"Socks help, too," said Paige.

"Actually," said Naira, "if you really want to be warm, what you should wear is a hat." She pointed to her own floppy one. "Eighty percent of your body heat escapes through your head, you know."

Leave it Naira to say something like that. She takes all these advanced science classes and stuff, and she's planning on being a doctor someday.

"Yeah, I guess," I said.

Maybe Naira was right about the hat. One time Heather, the captain of our cheerleading squad in Laurel Beach, got this idea that we should all wear little green berets to match our uniforms. She'd seen the berets in some cheerleading catalogue. Those catalogue people couldn't have had Florida cheerleaders in mind. The first and only time we tried wearing them at a game, we were totally boiling in about ten minutes.

Paige, Naira, and I arrived at the Cocoa

Bean. The second we were there, Jordan looked through the plate-glass window at us and waved. Sometimes it seems like he's got some kind of "Paige radar" or something. But I guess it's just that Paige and Jordan are super close.

I pulled open the heavy glass door, and we walked inside. The Cocoa Bean is one of the things I love about living in New York. It's totally adorable, with its little round green marble tables. And it's always busy and crowded. And it's one of the best places to spot cute guys.

"Well, if it isn't my favorite customers," said Jordan with a smile. He leaned over and gave Paige a quick kiss. "Table by the window, ladies?" he said, glancing at me.

I smiled. Jordan knows that when Cassandra and I come here alone, we always try to sit near the window. That way we can check out the guys both *inside* the Cocoa Bean and *outside* on the street at the same time.

I had the feeling a window seat didn't mean quite the same thing to Paige and Naira, though. After all, Paige already had a boyfriend. And Naira's got this really good friend who's a guy. At least, she *says* that's all they are. But sometimes I get the feeling that Chris wishes they could be more. Maybe Naira's just too busy to notice it. After all, she manages to handle a full course load, do really well in school, and have time for modeling, too.

Paige, Naira, Cassandra, and I all go to HSPS, the High School for Performing Students. They've got this special program where you can take only two academic classes if you want. I decided to do it so I could keep a lot of time free for modeling. And believe me, even going only half-time, I'm as busy as I could want to be.

Jordan showed us to our seats and took out his order pad. He looked at Paige and then Naira.

"The usual?" he said.

"Yeah, thanks, Jordan," said Naira.

Paige nodded.

Those two always have the same things when they go to the Cocoa Bean—a choco-cappuccino for Paige, and a regular coffee for Naira. I always like to try something new.

I studied the menu. "Mmmm, hazelnut crunch, that sounds good. What's that, Jor?"

"A cup of hazelnut-flavored coffee served

with a paper-thin cinnamon wafer on the side," Jordan recited with an English accent.

"Sounds good," I said. "I'll have one of those."

"You got it," said Jordan, scribbling on his pad. He picked up our menus. "Be back in a minute or two."

Paige put her jacket on the back of her chair. "Hey, Naira," she said, "did you do the math homework yet?"

Naira nodded. "I finished it last night."

"Boy," I said, "you don't waste any time, Ni. I never start my weekend homework until Sunday."

Naira shrugged. "It just makes sense to get it over with," she said. "That way, you don't have to think about it for the rest of the weekend. And it can't mess up your plans or any other things that might come up, like bookings."

"I guess," I said.

Naira turned to Paige. "Were you having trouble with the math homework?"

"Yeah," said Paige. "Remember the problem where we were supposed to find the value of x, where x was equal to y squared, and…"

Right away I began to space out. Like I said, Naira's great in school, and she's totally into science and math and stuff. Personally, I don't understand why anyone would find that *x* and *y* mumbo jumbo at all interesting. I mean, maybe if math used real things, instead of just letters...

Just then, I spotted Cassandra coming in the door of the Cocoa Bean. She was dressed in black jeans and a black leather jacket. The all-black outfit looked incredible with her dark hair and eyes. She saw me from across the room and waved excitedly.

Cass is my best friend here in New York. But she's not like *anyone* I knew at home in Laurel Beach. For one thing, she's from Brazil, so she speaks both Portuguese and English. And she's super sophisticated. She dresses totally cool, and she even had her own TV talk show in Brazil. But of all the girls I live with, Cass is the person I relate to the most. Somehow, even though our backgrounds are different, we're really similar in a lot of ways.

Cassandra hurried over to our table. "I *thought* I might find you guys here," she said, pulling up another chair. She sat down.

Naira looked up from the napkin where she'd been writing out her explanation of the math problem to Paige. "Oh, hey, Cassandra," she said.

"Hi," said Paige.

"Hi," said Cassandra. She pulled off her jacket and hung it on the back of the chair. "So, how was the shoot?"

"Pretty good," I answered. "Will Nichols shot the ad."

"Oooh, great," she said.

Will Nichols is one of Cassandra's and my absolute favorite photographers. He's super nice, and he knows how to bring out the best in you, which really shows up in the pictures. We both love working with him.

Just then, Jordan came over with our order.

"Hello, Cassandra," he said. He placed our mugs on the table. "Can I get you a *cafezinho*?"

Cafezinho is some special coffee from Brazil that Cassandra adores. I tried it once, but I don't get what the big deal is. To me it just tasted like it was made with way too much coffee and not nearly enough water.

Cassandra nodded. "Great, Jordan." When he walked away she looked around at all of us. "And now," she said, "the reason I came here to find you guys. I have *fantastic* news."

"Oh?" said Naira, raising an eyebrow.

"What is it?" I asked.

Cassandra paused dramatically for effect. Then she leaned even closer, her dark eyes sparkling.

"Well," she said, "while you were at the shoot, Jill Murray called."

"Oh yeah?" I said. "What's up?" Jill Murray is our booker at Ford. She keeps us up to date on anything we've been scheduled for.

Cassandra smiled. "We have just gotten a really cool booking."

"We?" said Paige. She looked around the table. "You mean all four of us?"

"I mean all *six* of us," said Cassandra. "Pia and Katerina have it, too."

"That's great," said Naira.

"Cool," I said. Working with my housemates was always fun. "What's it for?"

"*Style* magazine," said Cassandra. "They're doing a special Summer Fashion Forecast, and they want to use us."

"Wow," said Naira. She fumbled in her bag for a moment and pulled out her huge black datebook. Naira never goes anywhere without that datebook. "When is it?"

Cassandra waved her hand. "Oh, I don't know, in a week or something. Anyway, the exciting part isn't *when* it is, it's *where* it is." She looked at me. "How do you feel about going home, Kerri?"

"You're kidding!" I said excitedly. "The shoot's in Florida? Where?"

"Where else?" said Cassandra. "The *hippest*, the *hottest*, the *best* spot in Miami— South Beach."

"Oh my gosh," I said. "This is so great!"

South Beach is what the southern part of Miami Beach is called. It's famous for its candy-colored hotels, cute boutiques, and chic restaurants. Ford Models' Florida office is located there. And not only is South Beach one of the hottest spots around for modeling, but tons of celebrities vacation there, too.

Of course, the very best part of all was that South Beach is only a couple of miles from Laurel Beach! I'd be right near home, which meant I'd get to see my family and friends for the first time since I had moved to New York.

Suddenly, my mind was racing. This was incredible—I'd be able to hang out with Jessa and Heather again. It would be just like old times! I couldn't wait to call everyone up and tell them the amazing news.

CHAPTER 2

When we got back to the apartment I asked Mrs. Hill, our chaperon, about the details of the South Beach trip. Mrs. Hill told me that Jill Murray had said that we'd be leaving on Thursday and staying until the next Monday.

Then I headed straight for the phone on the table by the white couch in the living room. I shooed away Paige's black-and-white cat, Scooter, sat down on the edge of the couch, and picked up the phone. As I did, I straightened out my legs and did a couple of leg-lifts.

People always complain that they don't have the time to exercise, but I've found that you can manage to squeeze it in if you try. The moment I get up, I try to do fifty sit-ups. Then I try to do another fifty sometime during the day. I keep a running count of how

14

many of each thing I've done as the day goes on—sit-ups, leg-lifts, deep knee bends, whatever. I always know how many I have left to get done before the day is over.

Staying in shape is super important to me. Not only for modeling, but for the way it makes me feel, too. I remember one time I sprained my ankle jumping a hurdle at a track meet. I couldn't work out for over two weeks. I thought I'd go completely nuts.

That was back in freshman year, when I did about a zillion sports. I guess I was having kind of a hard time at home...and I just joined everything I could think of to take my mind off it. That was the year my parents got divorced and my dad got remarried. I signed up for practically every team—track, soccer, swimming, softball, you name it. Eventually it got to be too much for me, so I quit everything but the swim team. And I kept on with cheerleading, of course, which is where Heather, Jessa, and I first got to be friends.

I dialed Heather's number and listened to it ring. I knew I should probably call my mom first, but I couldn't resist making this call right away.

I was pretty sure I'd find them both at

Heather's. Jessa and I always used to hang out there. Heather's family has a giant house with a huge swimming pool. And there were always cute guys around because her older brother, Jake, and his friends hung out there, too.

Heather picked up the phone on the third ring. There was a moment of static, so I could tell she was on the cordless by the pool. "Hello?"

"Hi, Heath?" I said. "It's me, Kerr."

"Kerri!" she said. "Hi! Hey, Jessa, it's Kerri calling from New York."

I could picture the scene easily—Heather, lying on a lounge in her pink bikini, her honey-colored hair in a ponytail and her sunglasses pushed up on her head. Jessa was probably combing out her waist-length brown hair with the latest romance paperback open beside her on her lounge. I used to lie out in the sun and work on my tan, too. But that was before I started modeling and realized how terrible it is for your skin. Now I can't even *think* about doing it.

"Kerri, how are you?" said Heather. "How's life up north?"

"Pretty good," I said. "But it looks like I might be coming south soon."

"What do you mean?" she asked.

"I'm coming down to Miami!" I said.

"You're kidding!" Heather exclaimed. "That's great. Jessa, Kerri's coming down to visit!"

"Well, it's not *exactly* a visit," I said. "I'm really coming down to work."

"Work?" she asked. "Oh, you mean modeling."

"Yeah," I said. "I have an assignment for *Style* magazine, and I'll be staying in South Beach."

"That's fantastic! You'll be right nearby," said Heather. "I can come down and get you anytime. I just got my license, and my parents got me this great new car."

"Cool," I said.

"Oh, Kerri," said Heather. "It'll be just like old times."

"I know," I said. "Isn't it great? I'm totally excited!"

"Me, too," said Heather. "When are you coming?"

"I'll be down Thursday," I told her. "And I'll stay for four days."

"Only four days?" she said, sounding a little disappointed. "Well, I guess we'll just have to make the most of every one of them. Hey, hang on a sec. Jessa wants to talk to you."

I said a quick hello to Jessa, who was also pretty excited to hear that I was coming down. Then I hung up the phone to call my mother.

My sister Casey answered the phone. Casey's a year older than me. She's in her senior year at Laurel Beach High. My other sister, Andie, goes to Miami University.

"Hello?" said Casey.

"Hi, Case," I said. "It's me."

"Hey, Kerri!" she said. "It's great to hear your voice. What's up, kiddo?"

"Don't call me that," I said.

"Sorry," she said, "I just forget that you're so grown-up now."

"Oh, stop it," I said. But I didn't really mind her teasing; it felt like home. "I'm coming down to visit for a few days. I've got a shoot for *Style* magazine in South Beach."

"Wow, that's great," she said. "We haven't seen you in forever. Gosh, Mom's going to be so happy."

"Is she there?" I asked.

"Nope," Casey answered. "She's out showing a house."

After my parents' divorce, my mom got her real estate license. Before that, she'd pretty much been a stay-at-home mom. It was great having her around when I was growing up, but I definitely think she's happier now that she's involved in something else, too. She loves taking people to look at houses.

"Okay, well, just tell her I called," I said. "And that I'm coming down Thursday."

"Thursday, cool," said Casey. "I can't wait to see you, kiddo."

She hung up before I could yell. But I laughed when I put the phone down. I entered the call to Heather and my call home in the long-distance phone log next to the telephone. Then I picked up the receiver again—this time to call my dad.

Just then, Cassandra hurried into the room.

"Hey, Kerri, can I use the phone?" she said. "I've just had this absolutely totally incredible idea."

"Well, okay, sure," I said. "Go ahead." In a way, I didn't really mind putting off my call to my dad. Whenever I call my dad's house my stepmother, Sloane, answers the phone. She's all right, I guess, but I've never been very comfortable with her. "What's your incredible idea?" I asked Cassandra.

Her dark eyes sparkled. "Okay, listen to this. I was thinking, just before I left Brazil to come to New York, I had this talk with Roberto Lemos, the producer of *Qual o lance?*"

I nodded. *Qual o lance?* was the name of the TV show Cassandra used to host in Brazil. It means "What's Happening?" in Portuguese.

"And he said how sorry they were to see me go, and how much they were going to miss me and everything," she said.

"Right, I know," I said.

Cassandra had told me the story about a million times. How the producers of the show had been *so* upset to hear she was leaving that they had almost canceled the show, but then at the last minute they had settled on a replacement instead. Of course, the replacement was nowhere near as good as Cassandra. At least that's what Cassandra implied when she told the story, and probably she was right.

"So," she went on, "I was just thinking. Maybe just because I'm not on the show doesn't mean I can't be on the show."

"Huh?" I said, confused. "Oh, Cass, you

don't mean you're going back to Brazil, do you?"

"*Ta brincando?* Are you kidding? Of course not," she said. "At least, not in *person*. But here's my great idea. What if I still did special segments for the show now and then?"

"You mean from America?" I said.

"Sure," she said. "Or from wherever I happen to be—you know, like when we travel for shoots or something. I could be a special roving reporter, covering what's chic and happening all over the place."

"You're right," I said with a nod. "That's a totally cool idea."

"That's what I thought," said Cassandra. "And I figured my first report could be from South Beach."

"South Beach?" I said. "That's a great idea."

"That's what I thought," she said. "It's perfect. It has fashion, glamour, celebrities—everything." She picked up the phone. "Anyway, I'm calling Roberto right now to see what he thinks."

Cassandra began dialing. I lay down on the floor to do some sit-ups, since I was only up to sixty for the day. As I started my sit-ups, Naira came into the room and sat down in one of the white chairs by the window. She opened a notebook and began to write.

"Hey," I said, still doing sit-ups, "I thought you did all your weekend homework on Fridays, Ni."

Naira looked up from her notebook. "I do," she said. "At least, I try to. This isn't homework. I'm making a list of things to pack for Thursday's trip."

"Oh," I said.

Naira's super organized. I've never been like that myself, except about exercising. Some people don't see how I can keep track in my head of how many of each exercise I've done for the day. But it just seems to come naturally to me. I guess people are best at what they care most about.

As I continued my sit-ups, I could hear Cassandra talking on the phone. Of course, it was all in Portuguese, so I didn't understand a bit of it. Cass is always saying she's going to teach me Portuguese, but somehow we never get around to it. Whatever she was saying, though, I got the feeling the conversation was going pretty well.

I was on sit-up number ninety-seven for the day when she hung up the phone.

"Well, it's all set!" she said. "You're looking at the new traveling reporter for Brazil's hottest talk show."

"Wow, Cass, that's great," I said, doing another sit-up.

"Congratulations, Cassandra," said Naira. "Is it the show you used to host?"

"That's right," said Cassandra. "And now I'm going to be doing special on-the-spot reports for it. Roberto, the producer, loved my idea. He even came up with this great concept for it. Get this—it's just me and a camera, nothing else."

"You mean you're going to do the filming?" I asked, doing my last sit-up.

"That's right," said Cassandra, smiling. "Basic production methods are *the* hot thing in TV and movies now. Roberto says he's going to send me a video camera, and then I can just send him back my tapes."

"Oh," I said. "I get it." It sounded like fun.

"What kinds of things are you going to report on?"asked Naira.

"Whatever I want," said Cass with a shrug. "Roberto said it's up to me. I guess he realizes I've got a nose for what's hot."

That's for sure. Cassandra always knows

what's in and what's not. She's the perfect person to do something like that.

"So," said Naira, "you'll be behind the camera instead of in front of it this time. I guess that'll be an interesting change for you."

Cassandra's face fell. As I realized what Naira had said, I could see why. Cass absolutely *loves* being in the spotlight. But Naira was right. If Cassandra was the one doing the taping, how could she appear on camera?

"*Que mal!* This is terrible!" exclaimed Cassandra.

"Yeah, that's not going to be any fun for you, Cass," I said sympathetically.

"Hey, maybe you should give it a chance," said Naira. "The way I see it, the person controlling the camera controls *everything*. Besides, you never know. You might like being a behind-the-scenes reporter."

But I doubted very much that Cassandra would ever enjoy being a "behind-the-scenes" anything.

CHAPTER 3

Two days later, I sat with my housemates in one of the conference rooms at *Style* magazine's headquarters, on the fifteenth floor of this super-tall office building.

We were leaving for South Beach in three days, and we'd all come to the magazine's offices for a fitting. A fitting is a special appointment for models to try on the clothes that they'll be wearing. Whoever's in charge of the shoot can figure out what fits and what doesn't, and even decide to make alterations if necessary. It's also a chance to see which pieces of clothing go best together, and which models look right in which outfits.

The conference room had a big blue couch against one wall. Cassandra, Pia, and Paige were sitting on it, and I was plopped on the gray carpet in front of it, cross-legged. I'm always more comfortable sitting on the floor. Naira was leaning against a wall, and Katerina was perched on the edge of a chair. Her back was completely straight as usual, and her wavy brown ponytail tumbled down behind her.

Katerina's got the most amazing posture. I think she used to be some kind of ballet dancer. At least, that's what Cassandra told me, and I think she got it from Paige. Paige is better friends with Katerina than the rest of us are. Not that Katerina makes it easy to be friends with her. She's super quiet and keeps to herself, which sometimes seems snobby.

All over the office were numbered shopping bags filled with clothes. Standing in front of us was a young, dark-haired man wearing a white shirt with the sleeves rolled up and gray pleated pants. He was holding a clipboard. Next to him was a woman with short blond hair and glasses, wearing a green knit dress.

"Hi, everyone," said the man. "I'm Alex Kaplan. Jackie Bennet, our fashion editor, is in Paris right now. I'm her assistant, and she's asked me to take care of things until she gets back." He turned to the woman next to him.

"This is Amanda Fagen, our stylist. She'll be going down to South Beach with us, too."

"Hi," said Amanda, smiling.

"Okay," said Alex. "We've got a lot of things to try on, so let's get started. This shoot is for a Summer Fashion Forecast, so you'll be wearing everything from cutoffs to evening dresses. We won't know for sure which of you will be used for which shots until after we see what fits and talk to Jackie. But she'll let you know everything when we get down there." He looked down at the clipboard in his hand. "First, the Rudolfo outfit. Who do you think, Amanda?"

Amanda surveyed the room.

Cassandra leaned forward on the couch and whispered in my ear. "*Puxa*, wow, Rudolfo. He's a great designer. I bet it's gorgeous. Hope I get to wear it."

I shrugged. That's one way Cassandra and I are different. She's totally into designer clothes, and *my* idea of a great outfit is one that's super comfortable. I guess I like comfortable clothes because I spend a lot of time in exercise gear. You can't always work out in a Rudolfo gown.

"Definitely the redhead for the Rudolfo," said Amanda. "That cream color will be great with her hair." She looked at Paige. "I'm sorry, what's your name?"

"Oh, uh, me?" asked Paige. "I'm Paige."

"Okay, Paige," Amanda said. She reached for a shopping bag and checked inside. "Go into the dressing room over there and try this on, would you?"

"Oh, well," sighed Cassandra.

Paige took the bag from Amanda and went through the door to the next room.

"Okay, meanwhile, bag number two, the blue-and-white stripes," said Alex. He nodded toward me and raised his eyebrows at Amanda.

"Yes," she said. She looked at me. "You're Kelly, right?"

"Kerri," I corrected her.

"Oh, right, Kerri," said Amanda. "Sorry." She grabbed the shopping bag marked #2 and handed it to me. "Go in with Paige and give this a try. This style's perfect for you."

"Okay, sure," I said, taking the bag from her. I walked across the room and knocked lightly on the door. "Paige, it's me. I'm coming in."

When I got inside, Paige was stepping into

a long, cream-colored gown with a halter top and little sparkly glass beads all over it.

"Wow," I said, as she fastened the halter strap behind her neck, "you look totally amazing."

The dress really was beautiful. Cassandra would especially love this dress. But Amanda had been right. The color was great with Paige's long red hair.

Just then the door opened, and Pia came in with a shopping bag.

"*Ciao, ragazze!* Hi, girls!" she sang out, swinging her shopping bag a little. "I am here to join with you in trying on." She stopped in her tracks. "Ah, *che bella!* Paige, you look beautiful in this dress!"

"Really?" said Paige. She wrinkled her nose and looked down at the dress.

I don't think Paige feels all that comfortable in some of the fancier stuff she models. Before she came to New York two months ago, she lived on a farm in Nebraska and she'd never modeled in her life.

"You really do look great," I assured her. "Go on out and show Alex and Amanda."

As Paige left, I pulled the outfit out of my own shopping bag. It was a pair of blue-and-white striped cropped pants and matching cropped T-shirt.

"Oh, this is cute," I said.

Pia looked over at me. "Ah, yes, it is very sailor-like. I think this look is soon to be very in style. And you see how the stripes of the pants are standing up, and the stripes of the shirt are lying down? These will be very, how do you say—*lusinghieri*—flattering."

Now that she mentioned it, I saw what she meant. The shirt stripes were horizontal, and the pants stripes were vertical. Leave it to Pia to notice something like that. She's totally into fashion. She even designs and makes a lot of her own clothes.

The outfit in Pia's bag turned out to be a yellow sleeveless minidress with a deep V neck in the front. I thought it looked great on her, but after she put it on she frowned a little.

"Ah, *che mal*, but this is not right," she said, looking down.

"What's the problem?" I asked her, stepping into my striped pants.

"*Niente*, nothing much," she said. "It is only that this shape of neck is not the best with the cut of my hair."

As I looked at her, I could sort of see what

she meant. Pia's hair used to be very long, but she had it cut very short soon after she got to New York. Now it's grown out a little but it's still short. It's a great hairstyle for her, partly because it makes her neck look so long and elegant. But with the low-cut V of the dress, her neck ended up looking a little *too* long.

And it turned out that she wasn't the only one who felt that way. When Amanda saw her, she frowned as well, and shook her head.

"No, I don't think that one's right for you," she said to Pia.

"I agree," said Alex. He looked at his clipboard. "Why don't we give her the pink polka-dot instead? Naira can try that one on."

Amanda and Alex loved the striped pants and shirt on me, and they fit perfectly. For the next hour and a half, we tried on outfit after outfit. I tried on a hot-pink minidress and a long sheer yellow dress with a lacy slip underneath. There was also a pair of blue-and-white polka-dot overalls, but Alex and Amanda weren't too crazy about the way they fit me, so they gave them to Naira to try. Instead they gave me a pair of really short white cutoffs and a white crocheted top that I wore over a silver bikini top.

The fanciest thing I tried on was a long, deep-purple evening gown with a slit up the side. It was a great dress. Even Naira loved it, but she loves practically anything that's purple. Amanda and Alex liked the dress, too, but it was loose in the waist, so they pinned it where they thought it should be taken in.

Last, we all tried on these neat sarongs and bracelets that matched. Sarongs are printed Polynesian fabrics that are kind of like giant scarves. You can wear them a bunch of different ways—tied around your waist as a skirt, twisted and wrapped around your chest as a halter top, or around your head as a head-dress.

Amanda and Alex weren't sure yet exactly how we would each be wearing our sarongs, but they did a great job of picking out which sarongs looked best on which models.

Naira's sarong had turquoise and white flowers. The colors looked great against her brown skin, and the turquoise picked up the color of her blue-green eyes. Then Amanda picked a whole bunch of silver bangles for her to wear with it.

The bold colors of Cassandra's red-and-yellow fish pattern totally set off her dark eyes and hair. To go with the sarong, she got chunky wooden bracelets painted yellow, red, and orange.

Paige's sarong, with its peach-and-white shell design, looked incredible with her red hair and peaches-and-cream complexion. The outfit was topped off with a gold cuff bracelet for each wrist.

Alex and Amanda chose a sarong with brown-and-cream palm trees for Pia, which made her look even more exotic than usual. Then they had her try on a brass arm bracelet that was shaped like a snake and wrapped around her upper arm. Luckily, it fit.

The blue-and-pink bird pattern of Katerina's fabric showed off her blue eyes and incredibly fair skin. It went with a set of delicate bracelets of pink coral and seed pearls.

My own lavender-and-dark-blue lizard print brought out my blue eyes. Amanda and Alex had a hard time finding bracelets they liked to match it, though. Then Pia suggested that they find some bracelets made of a special metal. She had a difficult time explaining it, but finally we all figured out what she was talking about.

"Yes," said Amanda, "I know what it is.

When titanium is oxidized it gets these wonderful magenta, blue, and green swirls. And you're right, Pia, oxidized bracelets would be beautiful with Kerri's sarong."

"Sounds great," said Alex.

Alex made a note, and finally we were done. All of our clothes were selected for the shoots. Alex and Amanda had piles of notes about alterations that had to be made and additional accessories that had to be found.

As we all headed back downstairs in the elevator, a shiver of excitement ran through me. Now that we had been fitted for our clothes, the South Beach trip seemed that much closer. I couldn't wait to go!

CHAPTER 4

"Ah, *che bello!* This is beautiful!" exclaimed Pia. She was gazing up at the facade of the Fairleigh Hotel.

"Yeah, it is, isn't it?" I agreed.

The four-story building was painted pink and yellow, trimmed with curving rows of lavender neon light. The double glass doors at the entrance were etched with dolphins and palm trees. A lavender neon light above them said FAIRLEIGH in curvy script. There was a restaurant on the first floor that extended out onto the open patio. The patio was filled with round tables with white tablecloths.

It was late Thursday morning, and we'd just arrived in South Beach. The six of us were standing in the warm Florida breeze on Ocean Drive, the street that runs along the beach. Alex and Amanda from *Style* were with us, as well as the zillions of suitcases and boxes that held the clothes for the shoot. Jackie Bennet, *Style*'s fashion editor, had come in from Paris on a flight the day before. She was supposed to meet us at the hotel.

I sighed happily. It was great to breathe in the warm Florida air again. The sky was totally blue, and there were palm trees swaying in the breeze. I felt right at home.

We all walked into the lobby, which had mirrored walls and a gray-and-white marble floor and was filled with potted palms.

"Okay, everyone," said Alex. "Wait here a sec while I have them ring Jackie."

He walked over to the curved gray reception desk.

"You know," I said to Pia, "all the hotels in this area are painted pastel. They always remind me of candy."

"It's so neat that they made them all look like that," said Paige.

"I know," I said. "Isn't it?"

"Actually," said Naira, "the hotel owners *have* to paint their buildings these colors."

I turned to her in surprise. "They do?"

Katerina frowned. "There are such rules in America?"

Naira nodded. "In special cases there are. These buildings are all a style of architecture called Art Deco. They're some of the only ones like this in the country. So to preserve them, they're only allowed to be painted in special Art Deco pastel colors." She looked at Cassandra. "You know, that might make an interesting subject for one of your video reports."

Cassandra made a face. "No offense, Naira, but I don't think anyone would be interested in *that*." She patted the padded black shoulder bag that held her video camera. "I'll be concentrating on the glamorous side of things. *Puxa!* Wow! Speaking of glamour, did you see who just walked out of the elevator?"

I turned around and saw the back of a well-muscled, dark-haired man, dressed in a white polo shirt and black jeans, walking toward the door. "No, who was it?"

Cassandra's dark eyes widened. "Devon Redmond!" she squealed.

"Oh my gosh!" said Paige, her eyes wide.

"Really? You're not kidding? *The* Devon Redmond?"

Cassandra nodded. "The one and only. And he looks even cuter in person than he does in the movies."

"How could I have missed him?" sighed Paige.

"Oh, I bet you'll get another chance to see him," said Naira. "He's probably staying here in this hotel."

"That's so cool," I said. I could hardly believe it. I was staying in the same hotel as Devon Redmond, the most popular, the most *gorgeous* movie star ever. Sometimes modeling's the greatest.

"He is *molto popolare*, very popular, in my country as well," said Pia.

"*Da*, yes, in Russia also," said Katerina quietly.

"Wow," I said. I was surprised. "You mean you guys have American movies over there?"

"*Certo*, of course," said Pia. "Only they are, how you say, *doppiati*, with the Italian voices instead. Then the voice and the mouth do not always match so well."

I giggled. Somehow, the idea of seeing an American movie star like Devon Redmond with an Italian voice coming out of his mouth seemed funny.

Just then, Alex walked up with a tall, thin, beautiful older woman with sleek dark hair pulled into a French twist. She was wearing a soft, dusty-rose-colored sleeveless blouse and a long, straight white skirt with a slit.

"Hello, everyone!" she said, smiling. "I'm so glad to see you all made it all right. I'm Jackie." She turned to Naira and put out her hand. "Hello, Naira, how are you?"

"Fine thanks," said Naira. I could tell she was impressed that Jackie knew who she was.

Jackie continued down the line, shaking everyone's hand and addressing each of us by name. I was impressed, too. Obviously Jackie had been studying our composite cards or something.

"Now, let's get you all settled into your rooms," said Jackie. "Alex, you brought all the information from the fitting?"

He held up a brown leather bag. "I've got it right here."

"Good," said Jackie. "Why don't you and Amanda and I meet with Leslie right away to see if we can organize the shooting schedule a little more." She turned to us again. "Leslie

LaMont is going to be our photographer. She's based right here in South Beach."

"Ah, *sì*," said Pia. "I have heard this name. She does many of the photographs for the Japanese designer, Kisho, no?"

"Yes, that's right. Leslie does wonderful work," said Jackie, smiling at Pia. Then she looked around at all of us again. "All right, now, we'll be on a pretty tight schedule, because we have a lot of clothes to shoot. I'll give you each a copy of the exact shooting schedule later this afternoon, so you know which of you is needed when. I do know right now that we'll need some of you this evening." She turned to Alex. "Alex, who do we have in the stripes?"

Alex consulted his clipboard.

"Paige, Cassandra, Katerina, and Kerri," he read out.

"Okay, fine," said Jackie. "I'll need the four of you to meet me in the lobby at six-thirty tonight for a shoot at the marina. Meanwhile, Alex will give you each the number of the Ford Florida office down the street so you can check in for messages and things like that."

"So, does that mean we're all free for now?" asked Naira.

"That's right," said Jackie. "Oh, except for Pia and Paige. Amanda, I believe you said you had some questions about the alterations on some of their clothes?"

"Yes," said Amanda. "I just want to make sure that the green mini was taken up enough at the hem for Pia, and that the armholes on Paige's black-and-white striped dress are okay."

"Fine," said Jackie. "In the meantime, the rest of you are welcome to have lunch in the restaurant here, go for a swim across the street, relax, whatever. But if you're leaving the hotel, I'd like you to check in with Alex first and let him know. Alex, what's the situation with the rooms?"

Alex looked at a piece of paper in his hand. "They've got Naira, Paige, and Pia in 206. And 208 is for Kerri, Cassandra, and Katerina."

Cassandra shot me a quick look. I knew exactly what she was thinking. It was super that we were going to be staying together, but rooming with Katerina was going to be weird. She'd never been exactly friendly with either of us.

"Okay, then," said Jackie. "I'll see you four

at six-thirty sharp. Oh, and one more thing. Later on tonight, after the shoot, *Style*'s hosting a party down here in the restaurant. You're all invited, of course."

"Excellent," Cassandra whispered to me. "That could be my chance."

I knew just what she was thinking. "Maybe Devon Redmond'll be there," I said.

"Let's hope so," she said. "I'd love to snag an interview with him for my video report." Then she scowled. "That is, if I can think of a way to get *myself* into it, too."

Cassandra, Naira, Katerina, and I got in the elevator with Alex. The inside of the elevator was all silver with an amazing trim that had little cut-outs around its edges.

Once we were on the second floor, Alex gave us our room keys. I unlocked the door to room 208 and pushed it open.

The room was decorated totally in blue. There was blue wall-to-wall carpeting and three beds with blue spreads on them. An expanse of wide windows at the far end looked out over Ocean Drive. On the other side of the street, in the park by the beach, I could see the curving pink cement of the promenade filled with people strolling, skateboarding, and riding bikes. Beyond that was the sand and a shimmering stripe of blue—the ocean.

I walking over to the window. "This is the best," I said. It was great to be near the beach again.

Cassandra leaned on the windowsill next to me. "It sure is," she said. "Look, we're right above the front door. We've got a great view of anyone who comes in or out of the hotel."

She threw her suitcase on one of the beds and unzipped it. Then she began unpacking the zillions of things she had brought.

I laughed. "Cass, you look like you're ready to stay a *month*."

Katerina sat down on the end of one of the beds and switched on the TV. She watches a lot of TV. Pia, who rooms with her back in New York, had told me that Katerina had just bought a little portable TV for their room. Pia said that it "drove her to nuts" because it was on practically all the time.

Katerina picked up the remote and began flipping through the channels. I was sort of waiting to see what she would finally settle on—a talk show, a soap opera, a game show, reruns of an old sitcom—but it seemed like she was just going to keep switching around, channel surfing. Guys seem to do it all the time, but this was the first time I'd ever seen a girl channel surf.

Just then, the phone rang. I picked it up. It was my dad.

"Hey, there, Kerri," he said. "I'm glad I caught you."

"Hi, Dad," I said. "Yeah, we just got here. What's up?"

"Listen," he said, "how'd you like to go to lunch with your old man?"

I thought a moment. When Jackie had said we had the afternoon free, my first idea had been to call Heather and Jessa. But I guessed I could have lunch with my dad and still see them, too.

"Okay, Dad," I said. "Sure."

"Terrific," he said. "Do you know where Ruelle is?"

"Yeah," I answered. Ruelle is this great French restaurant on Ocean Drive. "I'm about three blocks away from there right now."

"Fine," he said. "I'll meet you there in half an hour. I'll give Sloane a call and let her know, too."

My heart sunk. I'd kind of been hoping

that it would be just me and my dad for lunch. But I didn't say anything. I know my dad has this thing about me and my sisters getting along well with Sloane. He's got some idea that we should all be best buddies or something.

"Okay, Dad, sure," I said. "See you then."

As soon as I hung up, the phone rang again.

"Hello?" I said.

It was Naira. "Hi," she said. "Kerri?"

"Yeah, hi, Ni," I said. "What's up?"

"I'm heading downstairs for lunch. Do you guys want to come?" she asked.

"I'm going out with my dad, but thanks anyway," I said. I turned to Cassandra and Katerina. "Do either of you want to go eat with Naira downstairs?"

"Definitely," said Cassandra. She was holding up a sleeveless white minidress and looking at herself in the mirror on the closet door. "I was planning on hanging out there all afternoon." She raised her eyebrows and grinned mischievously. "Devon Redmond has to get hungry sometime."

"*Da*, yes, I think I will go also," said Katerina quietly.

"Okay, Ni," I said. "You've got two takers."

"Great," said Naira. "I'll stop by in a couple of minutes."

When I hung up the phone, Katerina muted the television and turned to me. "May I ask you, please, Kerri, what is the meaning of this expression you used?"

"What expression?" I said.

"When you were on the telephone," she said. "In both of the conversations, you asked, 'What is up?'"

"Oh," I said. "'What's up?' It means, you know, 'What's new?' Or, 'What's going on?'"

"Okay," said Katerina. "So it does not have anything to do with something that is *up*, then. Is that correct?"

"You mean like *up* in the sky?" I said. I was trying not to laugh. "No."

"I see," she said quietly.

There was a knock on the door.

"You guys ready?" Naira called.

"Almost," Cassandra answered.

I was surprised at *that*. Cass usually takes forever to get dressed for anything. But I guess she really wanted to get downstairs fast.

"See you later, Kerri," she said. She opened the door. "Have fun with your father."

"Yes, good-bye," said Katerina, following her.

"See you guys," I called.

As they stepped into the hall, I heard Katerina say, "Hello, Naira. What is up?"

I shook my head. Katerina was so weird. I just couldn't understand her.

I looked at my watch. I still had twenty minutes before I had to meet my dad. So I decided to call Heather's house, but there was no answer there. I tried Jessa's next.

Her mother picked up the phone. "Wallace residence."

"Hi, Mrs. Wallace," I said. "This is Kerri."

"Kerri!" she said. "Well, how nice to hear your voice again. Are you in Miami? Jessa said you were coming to town."

"Yeah," I said. "I'm here for a shoot. Is Jessa there?"

"Why, no, dear," she said. "She's at school."

"Oh," I said. "Right."

How silly of me. Of course she and Heather would be at school on a Thursday in the middle of the day. I'd forgotten what day it was. Modeling schedules are pretty irregular, and since we don't go to school when we're working, I lose track of what other

47

people are doing sometimes.

"If you give me your number, I'll tell her to give you a call when she gets in," said Mrs. Wallace.

"Thanks," I said. Then I had a thought. "No, never mind, that's okay."

Because suddenly I remembered exactly where Jessa and Heather would be once school let out.

CHAPTER 5

"Thanks, Dad. It was great," I said as we all walked out of the restaurant into the sunshine.

"I do *love* French food," agreed Sloane.

"So, Kerri," said Dad, "how does it feel to be a tourist in your own hometown?"

I laughed. "It's okay, I guess."

"Where are you off to now?" he asked. "Back to the hotel?"

"Well," I said, "I was hoping that maybe you'd give me a ride over to Laurel Beach...I thought I'd go see some friends."

My father looked at his watch. "No can do, honey. I have a meeting in downtown Miami in fifteen minutes. But Sloane's headed that way, aren't you, Sloane?"

"Sure thing, Kerri," said Sloane. "I'd be glad to give you a ride."

49

"Uh, okay, thanks," I said.

We all walked over to the parking lot. Dad got into his car and I climbed into the passenger seat of Sloane's red sedan.

Sloane slid into the driver's seat. "Well, it must feel good to be back in the Florida sunshine," she said cheerily.

"Yeah," I said. "It sure does."

I looked over at her. She was wearing white pants and a turquoise blouse, and her streaked blond hair was pulled off her face with a gold barrette. Sloane isn't so bad, I thought. I even felt kind of sorry for her at that moment. She probably wasn't any more comfortable with me than I was with her.

Twenty minutes later, we drove into Laurel Beach. We passed by the high school. As I gazed out at the green lawns and sprawling redbrick buildings, my heart did a kind of a flip-flop. Suddenly it was totally weird to think that Jessa and Heather had started junior year without me.

We passed the football field, with its green-and-white banner that read GO LIONS!, and I thought of all the games I'd cheered at the year before. The Laurel Lions were the best team in the area—they'd won the regional championship three out of the past five years. We always liked to think the cheerleaders were part of the reason.

As we came into downtown, I checked my watch. It was three-fifteen—perfect. School had let out fifteen minutes ago.

We drove past the Laurel Beach Cinema and Something Special, Jessa's mother's gift shop. Even though I'd only been gone a couple of months, somehow it felt like a lot longer. So much had happened since I had moved to New York. My life was so different now.

"Where can I drop you, Kerri?" asked Sloane.

"Um, right up ahead, at Pop's, please," I told her.

Pop's was the Laurel Beach High hangout. Everybody went there after school. The year before, Heather, Jessa, and I had practically *lived* there.

"Bye, Sloane," I said as I opened the car door. "Oh, and thanks for the ride."

"See you soon, I hope," she answered. She smiled cheerfully, and I felt a bit guilty as she drove away.

I walked in the door to Pop's, and the familiar smell of burgers and fries hit my nose. Suddenly it was as if I'd never left. The juke-box was playing, and the counter and tables were filled with kids.

Then I heard someone call out my name. I turned and saw a couple of football players sitting at a table nearby.

"Hey, Kerri, how you doing?" called one.

"Pretty good," I called back, waving.

I made my way through the room and people kept calling out to me. I wanted to stop and talk, but I just waved and kept going. I was in a hurry to get to the booth in the far corner. That was our booth—mine, Heather's and Jessa's.

Sure enough, there they were. And they hadn't spotted me yet. It looked like Heather must be telling some kind of funny story, be-cause she was waving her arms in the air and making faces. Jessa was sitting next to her, leaning against her and laughing.

Heather saw me first. Her big blue eyes grew even bigger, and she jumped up.

"Oh my gosh! Kerri!" she shrieked.

"Hi, you guys!" I said, running over.

"You're here!" exclaimed Jessa.

I couldn't believe how good it made me

feel to see their familiar faces—Heather's bouncy blond ponytail and the freckles on her nose, Jessa's big brown eyes and long, silky brown hair.

Jessa slid out of the booth, too, and for a moment the three of us just looked at each other. Then we all sort of collapsed into one big hug. I could tell that people were staring, but I didn't care at all. It felt great. We sat back down in the booth, and they looked at me.

"Wow, Kerri," said Heather. She took a sip of her milk shake. "You look great."

"But you're so pale!" wailed Jessa. "It's like you're a real Northerner now or something."

I laughed. "Don't worry, I'm still a Florida girl inside," I said. "But I can't lie out in the sun now, anyway. You know, I'm supposed to take care of my skin."

"Oh," said Heather. She bit into a french fry. "You mean for modeling?"

I nodded.

"But you were modeling when you were down here, and you used to lie out," said Jessa.

"Only with sunblock on," I reminded her. "Besides, that was different. I mean, Sunshine

53

was just a local agency, and I was mostly modeling swimsuits anyway. Now that I'm with Ford it's more of a big deal. Besides, I'm used to it the way my skin looks untanned."

"See?" said Jessa, laughing. "I *told* you she was a real Northerner now."

We all laughed.

"Seriously though, Kerri," said Heather. "What's it like living in New York?"

"Really fun," I answered. "You guys should see the apartment my roommates and I live in. The living room's got all this cool white furniture in it, and I can see the river from my room."

"The river?" asked Jessa.

"Yeah," I said. "I think it's the East River. I'm still not that good at finding my way around. Luckily the Fords usually have someone to help us find our way to shoots and stuff."

Heather shook her head. "I still can't imagine you living in a big city, Kerri. Don't you miss the beach?"

"Yeah, I do," I admitted. "Sometimes when I'm swimming in the pool at Jolie, this spa I go to, I close my eyes and imagine I'm back here, in the ocean."

"A spa, huh?" said Jessa. "Sounds so glamorous."

I shrugged. "It's really just a fancy health club. And the pool's half the size of the one at Laurel Beach High. Still, it's fun. My friend Cassandra and I go there a few times a week. Cass gets facials and manicures and stuff like that. I mostly go to swim and take exercise classes."

Heather rolled her eyes. "Same old Kerri. Still exercising every minute."

"Hey, I have to keep in shape," I said. "For modeling."

Jessa tossed her hair a little. "Yeah, so do we," she said. "For cheerleading."

That's not quite the same thing, I thought. But I didn't say it.

"So, what's new with you guys, anyway?" I said instead. "What's happening these days at Laurel Beach High? Give me all the latest dirt."

Heather looked at Jessa. "Should I tell her?"

"Tell me what?" I said.

Jessa sighed. "Heather's in love."

I leaned forward eagerly. "Who's the guy?"

Heather smiled and her cheeks got pink.

"Steve Bishop," she said, sighing.

My heart skipped a beat. Steve Bishop had been new at Laurel Beach High the year before. He'd transferred from Nebraska or Nevada or somewhere. He was on the football team, but other than that he'd been kind of a loner. He had black hair and blue eyes. I'd secretly had a crush on him.

"Really?" I managed to say.

Jessa nodded. "They're quite an item. Show her the *ring*, Heather."

I swallowed. "He gave you a ring?"

Heather sighed and shook her head. "It's not a ring, Jessa, and you know it." She pulled a chain out of her pink T-shirt and showed me a little silver hoop at the end of it. "It's from his car keys. The first time we kissed, they were in his hand, and this piece of his key chain came off and got stuck in the back of my sweater." She smiled. "He was so cute. He untangled it and slipped it on my finger like a ring."

"That's sweet," I said. I had to admit, it did sound pretty romantic.

"What about you?" asked Heather. "Have you met any cute guys in New York?"

"No one special," I said, and grinned. "But

I'm having lots of fun looking. Cassandra and I like to go to this place called the Cocoa Bean. It's a great place to check out guys."

"Oh yeah," said Heather. "I think you told us about that place. It's a coffee shop, right?"

"Actually, it's a coffee *bar*," I told her.

"Well, excuse me, a coffee *bar!*" said Heather. "That sounds pretty fancy. I bet they don't make fries like Pop's does, though."

"They sure don't," I said. Pop's was famous for their fries.

"Here," said Heather, passing me her plate. "Have some."

"Well, okay," I said. "Maybe just one."

"Are you kidding?" she said. "No one can eat just one Pop's french fry."

I shook my head. "They're bad for my skin."

"Wow," said Jessa. "You're taking this stuff really seriously."

"Yeah, well, I have to," I said. "It's a big deal now, you know?"

"Hey, Kerri, you chose the perfect weekend to come down," said Heather, changing the subject. "The Lions are playing Freshwater on Saturday."

"Wow," I said.

Freshwater High was Laurel Beach's biggest rival. It was always a big deal when the Laurel Lions played the Freshwater Gators.

"And there's going to be a humongous party tomorrow night at the Jenkinses'," Jessa added.

The Jenkinses had four kids, all at Laurel Beach High. I knew one of them, Anne, from the swim team. They were famous for their great parties.

"Wow," I said. "It sounds great, but I'll have to check my schedule. The fashion editor for the shoot I'm supposed to be doing just got in from Paris, and she's still figuring out when she needs us to work."

"Oh," said Heather, "I get it. But you're not going to be working the *whole* time, are you?"

"Really," said Jessa. "We're still going to hang out and stuff like you said, right?"

"Oh, sure," I said, although I was beginning to wonder. I really had no idea how often Jackie would schedule me to work. I'd tried on zillions of clothes at that fitting in New York so I could be scheduled for a lot of sessions. But I put it out of my mind. After all, I was bound to have some free time.

"Don't worry," I said. "I'm sure it'll work out."

"Good," said Heather. "We've missed you, you know."

"Yeah," said Jessa. "Seeing you back here at Pop's just seems right, Kerri."

"Yeah, I know," I said. I felt the exact same way.

CHAPTER 6

It was a little after six o'clock by the time Heather had driven me back to South Beach in her new cherry-red sports car. At the hotel there was a message from my mother waiting for me. I felt bad that I hadn't called her yet, but now I barely had time to take a shower before I had to be downstairs in the lobby with Cassandra, Katerina, and Paige for the shoot. Besides, I knew Mom would understand.

Jackie was waiting for us in the lobby, along with an African-American woman with close-cropped hair, a tall blond man, and a heavyset woman with outrageous makeup on. Jackie introduced the first woman as Leslie LaMont, the photographer. The man, Brian, was the hairstylist, and the other woman was Natalie, the makeup artist.

Jackie had several cabs waiting outside. We all piled in and headed for the shoot location, which was the South Point Marina, at the tip of South Beach. Alex and Amanda were already there with the location vans containing all the clothes.

When we got to the marina, I could see why Leslie LaMont had chosen the early evening to shoot there. The sun was low in the sky, and the white boats were practically glowing as they bobbed gently in the still blue water. By sunset it would be totally gorgeous.

Since there were four of us to get ready, Jackie had Katerina and me get our makeup done first and Cassandra and Paige get their hair done first to save time. Katerina and I headed into one of the location vans with Natalie to get our makeup done.

"Okay, Katerina, let's start with you," Natalie said. She pointed to the small director's chair she had set up at one end of the van. "Sit."

"Excuse me, just one moment, please," said Katerina. She reached into the pocket of her jeans, took out a folded piece of paper, and handed it to me.

"You were not here when Alex came to give

these," she said. "So I have gotten one extra for you." She sat down on the chair.

I opened up the paper. It was the shoot schedule for the weekend.

"Hey, thanks," I said.

"Not problem," she said. She closed her eyes as Natalie began to apply her foundation.

Natalie grinned.

"Um, I think you mean 'No problem,'" I told Katerina.

I could see her fair skin reddening even under the foundation.

"Oh, yes, that is right," she said with her eyes still closed. "No problem." She repeated it a couple of times quietly, as if she were trying to memorize it. "No problem. No problem."

I smiled to myself. It was kind of cute the way Katerina worked so hard to learn phrases like "No problem" and "What's up?"—expressions that came so naturally to me.

I looked down at the schedule. There were at least two or three shoots for each day. The outdoor shoots were all either early in the morning or late in the day, like this one. I knew it was because photographers don't like to shoot outside when the sun is at its peak—especially in places like Florida, where the sun's super strong. Aside from the outdoor shoots there were also a couple of indoor studio sessions scheduled for the afternoons.

It looked like I was booked for shoots the following morning and afternoon, as well as Saturday and Sunday mornings. It was a pretty busy schedule, but it still left me time to do a few things with Heather and Jessa. It seemed as though I'd probably even be able to go to the big game against Freshwater on Saturday.

Natalie finished Katerina's makeup and called me over. I folded up the schedule and put it in the pocket of my cutoffs.

I sat down in front of Natalie and lifted my face. "Wow," she said, "you've got great skin."

"Thanks," I said.

"Really, it's just great," she repeated as she sponged foundation onto my face. "You must take good care of it."

"Yeah, I try," I said. I thought of the conversation I'd had earlier with Heath and Jess. Good skin seemed worth the trouble of staying out of the sun and keeping away from things like greasy french fries. But it certainly wasn't easy.

A little while later, I was ready to go. Natalie had finished my makeup and Brian had put my hair in a cute high ponytail with little tendrils around my face.

The theme of the shoot was stripes—*Style* was predicting that striped clothes were going to be very hot next summer. So we all wore striped outfits and white slip-on sneakers. I put on the blue-and-white striped pants and top I'd tried on at the fitting, along with a pair of sneakers.

Brian had tied Paige's curly red hair on top of her head in a loose knot with some ringlets hanging down. She wore a long sleeveless dress with diagonal black-and-white stripes. Amanda had given her a pair of white hoop earrings to wear.

Cassandra was in a white tank top and green-and-white striped short-shorts. She had a matching green-and-white striped head-band in her hair.

Katerina was dressed in a red-and-white horizontal-striped short-sleeved bodysuit with a flouncy blue miniskirt. Brian had put her hair in two adorable long braids with red, white, and blue striped bows at the end.

"Wow," said Paige, looking at her. "You look really all-American."

"You think?" said Katerina. Her face lit up.

"Sure," said Paige. "I mean, those are the colors of the flag. You almost look like you could be going to a Fourth of July picnic or something. All you need are some stars."

"Ah, yes," said Katerina. She nodded seriously. "Four of July. This is American Independence Day, yes?"

"That's right," I told her.

She nodded again. "I am very much looking forward to this important holiday."

Cassandra glanced at me and I shrugged. Katerina could be weird sometimes. So the Fourth of July is fun and everything, but it isn't *that* much of a big deal. Who knows, I thought, maybe she's just into fireworks or something.

Style had rented a gorgeous boat for the shoot, so we all climbed on board. Modeling's so cool—you get to hang out in these great places that you wouldn't normally even get to see. The boat *Style* had rented was a giant yacht. You know, the kind that are practically like a house, with bedrooms and a kitchen and everything. Painted across the side was the name ISLAND HOPPER.

The boat impressed me, but the best thing about it was the guy *Style* had hired to sail it.

He was incredibly cute, with short brown curls and an amazing body with huge muscles.

"Mmmm," said Cassandra, as we climbed on board. "I wouldn't mind doing some 'island hopping' with *that* guy."

"That's for sure," I said.

Just then, the guy turned toward us. For a moment, I froze, thinking maybe he'd heard us talking. But he just smiled.

"Hi," he said. "I'm Chuck."

"Hi," said Cassandra in a breathy voice. "I'm Cassandra."

I shook my head. I'd always thought that *I* was a flirt. But that was before I met Cass. She flirts with practically every guy she meets.

It turned out that Chuck's job was to drive us around and around and around the harbor. Meanwhile, Leslie was going to try to shoot us with the open sea in the background, so it would look like we were way out in the water.

"We only have this light for a little while, so let's work fast," said Leslie.

"Fine," said Jackie. "I'd like to do Kerri, in the blue, and Cassandra, in the green, together. Don't you think, Amanda?"

"Yes," said Amanda. "I agree."

"Let's do it," said Leslie. "Girls, I'd like you to stand over there, by that railing."

Cassandra and I made our way over to the edge of the boat. There was a short white railing running around the deck.

"Okay, fine," said Leslie. "Now, let's see, Cassandra, put your hands on your hips and face me. That's it. Now, Kerri, stand next to her, maybe with your back to her, and sort of look out over the water."

I moved next to Cassandra and adjusted myself the way Leslie had said.

"Great," said Leslie. She peered through her camera. "Now, cheat your body a little toward me if you can."

I twisted slightly in her direction.

"Perfect," she said. The shutter started clicking.

For the next few minutes, Leslie shot Cassandra and me together, varying our poses a bit. Even though we were wearing sneakers, it was a little hard to balance on the boat like that while it was moving. Luckily we weren't going too fast.

Every once in a while, I'd sneak a peek at Chuck as he steered the boat. I could tell Cassandra was doing the same thing. I almost always know exactly what she's thinking, which is one of the reasons I love working with her. When you model with someone else, the chemistry between you can be important. Cass and I are definitely on the same wavelength. Sometimes after we've been holding a pose a while and it begins to feel a little stale, we'll both shift into a new pose at exactly the same moment.

After Leslie finished a couple of rolls of film, she shot some of Paige and Katerina together. Then we all sat on the edge of the boat, swinging our legs over the side.

Before we knew it, the sky was getting dark and the pastel neon lights of the South Beach hotels started to glow back on shore. I began getting excited about the *Style* party at the Fairleigh later that evening.

It had already been a long day. But it had been a great day, too. Seeing Heather and Jessa had been really fun. And the shoot had gone well. Now tonight I'd be going to a glamorous party. Modeling can just be the best.

CHAPTER 7

"Hi, Mom!" I said into the phone. "It's me."

"Kerri!" said my mother. "How nice to hear your voice, sweetie. I've been trying to reach you, you know. Did you get my messages?"

"Yeah," I said, feeling a pang of guilt. My mom had called again while I was at the marina shoot. "I've just been *really* busy."

"Oh, of course, honey, I understand," she said. "After all, you are down here to work. But tell me, when *are* we going to see you? Do you have any time off at all?"

"A little," I said. I thought of the schedule in my pocket. I wanted to see my mom, but I wasn't too sure when I could. Maybe sometime between the shoot and seeing my friends...

"Well, just let me know," said my mother.

"Okay, Mom, I will," I said. I looked at my watch. "I've gotta go right now, though. There's this party downstairs the magazine wants us to go to, so I need to get ready."

"All right, honey," said my mother. "But give me a call soon, okay?"

"Sure, Mom," I said. "I will."

"Come *on*, Cass, let's go," I sighed forty-five minutes later.

"Okay, wait just one more minute," she said. She was scrutinizing herself in the full-length mirror for the zillionth time. "I'm just not sure that I like this outfit. I think I want to change."

I groaned. "No, Cass, *please*, not again!" I sat down on the bed and shook my head. For someone who usually knew what she wanted, Cass had a harder time getting dressed than anyone I'd ever met before in my life. She'd already changed her entire outfit four times. Now it looked like she was taking off the silver minidress with skinny spaghetti straps and putting back on the first thing she'd tried on, a short, straight black dress with four straps across the back that came together at a silver metal ring in the center.

I looked down at my own white silk knit tank dress. There hadn't been much question about what I would wear. It was the only nice dress I'd brought with me to Florida. And I almost hadn't even packed that, but Cassandra had talked me into it.

Katerina was wearing an off-the-shoulder peach brocade dress with a short full skirt. She was sitting quietly on her bed, reading what looked like some kind of magazine. I wondered why she didn't just go down to the party. Could she be waiting to go with us?

Cassandra changed back into the black dress and was touching up her burgundy lipstick in the mirror. Then I thought of the perfect way to get her to leave. In fact, it was probably the *only* way.

"You know, Cass," I said casually, "I was just thinking—a busy celebrity like Devon Redmond might have more than one party to go to in a night. What if he stops by this one first? I mean, since he's right in the building and everything."

She turned to look at me.

"*Puxa,* wow, you're right," she said. "I didn't even think of that. Come on, we'd better get down there before he leaves."

I smiled to myself. I've gotten to know Cassandra really well.

I turned to Katerina. "Are you coming?"

"*Da.* I mean, yes," she said.

She tossed her magazine on the bed. I noticed it wasn't a magazine at all but a comic book, a *Jody & Jimmy* comic. I recognized it right away because I used to read them. Jody and Jimmy were a typical all-American high school couple. But I hadn't read *Jody & Jimmy* since I was ten! I shook my head. Katerina was full of surprises.

We walked down the hall and took the silver elevator to the first floor. Then we went into the Fairleigh's restaurant, which had been closed to the public for the party.

The moment we walked in the door, Cassandra's eyes began darting around. I looked around, too, but I didn't see Devon Redmond anywhere.

"Oh, well," she said, sighing. "Maybe he'll show up later."

A bank of tables over by the far wall was covered with white tablecloths. On top of the tables were three huge flower arrangements and platters of food. There were flowers all over the huge, curved silver bar as well. Waiters in black T-shirts and white jackets were milling around with trays, serving drinks and appetizers.

As I looked at everything, I thought about how much my life had changed in the past few months. Last summer, I'd been a regular Laurel Beach cheerleader, hanging out with my friends. Sure, I'd done a little local modeling in my spare time, but before I'd moved to New York, I'd never been to a party like this. I thought about Heather and Jessa. They'd be totally impressed if they were here.

The restaurant was already filled with people. I could see several familiar faces. A few of them were familiar because I knew them, like Jackie and Leslie, but there were also a lot of really famous people there—people whose faces I'd seen on TV and in magazines.

It's weird, though, how I *knew* they were famous but wasn't sure about exactly who they were. Sometimes that happens to me. I see a face, and I know I've seen it about a zillion times before...but I just can't put a name with it.

That's another reason I love hanging around with Cass. She always knows who everyone is at this kind of party. Even the people who are only sort of famous. I guess that's partly because she reads this newspaper called *Buzz*, which tells all about what the hippest New York party people are up to.

I turned to her.

"Hey, Cass," I said, "who's that woman over there by the wall?"

I nodded toward an incredibly tall, dark-skinned woman in a red dress who was talking to a short, bald man in a suit.

"That's Leyla," she said.

I nodded. I *knew* she'd looked incredibly familiar. Leyla was one of Ford's hottest models. She had started out as a movie actress in Europe, and since Ford had taken her on she had signed an exclusive contract with La Dame cosmetics.

"And I just realized who that guy she's talking to is," said Cassandra.

"Who?" I asked.

"Mario Filippi, the Italian movie director!"

I shrugged. The name *sounded* familiar, but I still didn't really know who he was.

"Look," said Cassandra. "He's on his way to the bar. I'm going over there to see if I can start a conversation. Who knows? This could be really important for me."

Cassandra plans on being a famous movie star someday, as well as being a famous model and TV personality. If anyone else told me they wanted to be all those things, I'd laugh, but believe it or not, Cass can probably do it. She's totally driven when it comes to stuff like that.

As she headed toward the bar, she turned back to me one more time. "Don't forget to let me know if you see him," she said.

"You got it, Cass," I said. I didn't have to ask—I knew she meant Devon Redmond.

"Excuse me," said Katerina. "May I ask you something, please?"

I turned in surprise. I hadn't even realized that she was still standing next to me.

"Sure," I said. "What's up?"

She smiled. And when I realized what I had said, I smiled, too.

"When you are using the short version of the name, what is this called?" she asked.

"Huh?" I said. What was she talking about?

"The short version," she repeated. "I have noticed that you are often calling Cassandra 'Cass,' and Naira 'Ni.'"

"Oh," I said. Now I knew what she meant. "Those are nicknames."

"Nicknames," she repeated. "This is like the short version for Nikolai, I mean Nicholas, correct?"

"Hey, yeah, I guess so," I said. I had never really thought about it before, but maybe the name Nick was where that word had come from to begin with.

Just then, Naira came up to us.

"Hey, Ni," I said. "What's up?"

"Yes, Ni," said Katerina. "What is up?"

"Not much," said Naira. "How was the shoot?"

"Fun," I said. "What did you guys do?"

"Oh, Pia and I went shopping," she said. "There are some great vintage clothing stores around here. Pia was in heaven."

"Are you booked for that shoot tomorrow morning?" I asked.

"I think we all are," said Naira. "Alex said we're doing the sarongs."

"Cool," I said. I liked the sarongs. "Hey, I think I'm going to go get a glass of mineral water or something. Do you guys want anything?"

Naira shook her head. "No, thanks, I'm fine."

"No, thank you," said Katerina.

I made my way up to the silver bar. There was already a pretty big crowd there. I had some trouble getting the bartender's attention.

"Hey, maybe I can help. What are you having?" said a voice next to me.

I turned and saw a tall guy with slicked-back dark hair, wearing a black jacket with a dark green shirt buttoned up to the collar.

"Oh," I said, "a mineral water."

He caught the bartender's eye. "Two mineral waters, please."

"Thanks," I said as he handed me the glass.

"My pleasure," he said. "So, what brings you to this party? Are you with Ford?"

I nodded.

"Me, too," he said. He put out his hand. "Claude."

"Kerri," I said, shaking it.

I wasn't surprised to hear that he was a model. He was very good-looking, even if he wasn't my type. I go for the all-American, athletic look. Like Steve Bishop, I thought with a sigh, remembering the little ring Heather had had on her neck. Claude was lankier and more sophisticated-looking.

Claude looked at me a moment.

"That's funny," he said.

"What?"

"It's just that you don't really look familiar," he said. "I thought I knew all my fellow Ford Florida models."

"Oh," I said, "I'm not with Ford Florida. I'm with the New York agency."

"Well, that explains it," he said. He smiled. "So, what brings you down to sunny Florida, Kerri?"

"Actually, I'm here on a booking," I told him. "A shoot for *Style*. We'll be here until Monday."

"Maybe we could get together while you're here," said Claude. "You know, I could kind of show you around Miami."

I smiled. "Actually, I'm *from* Miami."

His face reddened a little. "Oh, you are?"

"Yeah," I said. "Are you?"

"No," he said. "I mean, not originally. I'm from Cleveland."

"Cleveland," I said. "That's in Iowa, right? Or Idaho?"

"Ohio," he corrected.

I shrugged. "Whatever. Where'd you get a name like Claude? Isn't that a French name or something?"

He blushed some more. "Well, I'll tell you a secret," he said. "It wasn't *always* Claude. Originally it was Clyde. Clyde Ledbetter. I was named after my grandfather. I changed it when I started with Ford. Somehow Clyde just didn't seem like the right name for a model."

"I guess," I said, shrugging again.

Just then, Pia came rushing up to us. She was wearing a simple white dress embroidered all over with yellow sunflowers. I knew she had probably done the embroidery herself.

"Ah, *che fortuna*, what luck!" she said excitedly. She looked at Claude. "Oh, *scusami*, excuse me for interrupting. It's just that I cannot believe what has just happened to me." She sighed happily. "Oh, Kerri, I have gotten to *meet* him. He has actually spoken to me!"

"Who?" I said. I looked around wildly. "Devon Redmond?" If he was there, I had to find Cassandra right away and tell her.

"Who?" said Pia. "Oh, no, not him. This was even more exciting—at least for *me*." She looked at me. "I have gotten to meet Pierre Fouchy."

"Pierre Fouchy?" I said. It sounded familiar. Then because it was Pia I realized it must be a designer. "The designer?"

"But of course!" said Pia. "Is there another?"

"No," I said, shaking my head, remembering that Pierre Fouchy was one of the world's biggest designers. But only Pia would think it was more exciting to meet a French fashion designer than an American movie star.

"Pia, this is Claude," I said.

"*Piacere,* nice to meet you," said Pia. She shook his hand.

"Same here," said Claude. "So, you're into fashion, huh?"

"*Sì,*" said Pia, nodding. "Very much. I wish to be a designer myself someday."

"Really?" said Claude. "That's very interesting, because…"

I wandered off, leaving them to their conversation. I wondered where Cassandra was. I hadn't seen her in a while. I supposed she must be pretty disappointed that Devon Redmond had never shown up.

Just then I saw her rushing into the restaurant from the lobby. She had a huge grin on her face. I saw her scanning the crowd, so I waved. She hurried over to me and grabbed my arm.

"I have to find Naira right away!" she said.

"Why?" I said. "What's up?"

"Oh, Kerri, you'll never believe it," she said. "I met him. And I spoke to him!"

"You're kidding?" I said. "You mean Devon Redmond?"

She nodded, her eyes shining.

"But where is he?" I said, looking around. "I've kept an eye out for him all night. I didn't see him anywhere at the party."

"He didn't come to the party," she said.

"Then, how did you meet him?" I asked.

"In the elevator," she said. "You see, I ate a shrimp puff and I thought it might have smudged my lipstick. But when I went to touch it up, I realized I had left my lipstick upstairs. So I figured I'd just run up to the room for a moment and get it. And guess who I ran into in the elevator!"

"Wow, Cass, that's great," I said. "But why are you looking for Ni?"

"Well," she said, "I had to think of *something* to talk to him about to break the ice, so I rode up to the fourth floor with him—that must be where he's staying, I guess they put him on the top floor because he's such a big celebrity—and I made some comment about the elevator. You know, how it's all silver and everything."

I nodded.

"So," she went on, "it turned out that he's really into the whole Art Deco style thing that Naira was talking about—you know, how all the buildings around here are this one style, and they have to paint them certain colors and stuff?"

"Yeah?" I said.

"He said that's the main reason he comes down here," she said. "He's a member of some South Beach preservation board called Save the Splendor or something. So I pretended that I was really into it, too."

"Natch," I agreed.

"Anyway, here's the good part," said Cassandra. "I told him all about the TV show, and I said that I was *sure* my viewers would be fascinated by what he and his group were doing down here to preserve the architecture. And he said he'd be willing to meet with me tomorrow afternoon to talk about it!"

"And now you need a crash course on the whole thing from Ni," I finished.

"Right," she said.

"Okay," I said, "I'll help you look around for her. But first I have a question, Cass."

"Sure," she said. "What?"

"How did you ever manage to get all of this information out of Devon Redmond in such a short elevator ride?"

She smiled. "Hey, I guess I just have the touch for these things. Imagine what I could have gotten out of him if we were staying in a taller hotel!"

We both burst out laughing.

CHAPTER 8

"All right, Kerri, let's try yours like this," said Amanda, holding up the lavender-and-dark-blue lizard-print sarong.

I lifted my arms, and she folded the large piece of fabric in half and wrapped it around my waist like a miniskirt, knotting it at my hip.

"There," she said, standing back. "That looks great. I found the bracelets that Pia talked about, the oxidized ones, and they match perfectly. Why don't you try on that white bikini top over there? Then you can add the bracelets."

It was early Friday morning. I was getting dressed in one of the location vans that was parked near the beach. Natalie had already done my makeup, and my hair was still up in the hot rollers Brian had set it in.

I eased my red tank top over my head so I could slip into the white bikini top. Meanwhile, Amanda was knotting Pia's brown-and-cream sarong into a long, strapless dress.

"*Ma che straordinario!* How amazing is this garment," said Pia, looking down at the sarong. "It is only one piece of cloth, and yet it can be so many things!"

"I know," said Amanda. "Jackie thinks they're going to be very in this summer because they're so versatile, which makes them economical, too. All you have to do is buy one and you can get lots of outfits out of it."

Pia nodded. "*Sì, capisco*, I understand," she said.

I had to admit, now that I was actually wearing one, I was starting to have my doubts about the sarongs. They were super pretty and everything, but they also seemed a little too exotic to be very practical. I mean, I couldn't exactly imagine Heather or Jessa walking around Laurel Beach High dressed like this. I couldn't imagine walking around New York in one, either. But Amanda and Pia knew a lot more about fashion than I did, so I wasn't about to say anything.

A burst of static came out of the walkie-talkie on the table nearby. Amanda picked it up. Sometimes people working on a shoot use walkie-talkies so they don't have to keep running back and forth between the set and the location vans.

"This is Amanda," she said, speaking into it.

"Alex here," said the voice on the other end. "Jackie says to send the models out as you get them ready, okay?"

"Sure thing," replied Amanda.

Just then there was a knock on the door of the trailer.

"Kerri!" Brian called. "I think your rollers are ready to come out now."

"Coming!" I called.

I quickly tied the straps of the bikini top behind my neck. Amanda handed me a stack of magenta and blue titanium bracelets.

"Put them all on one arm," she instructed.

I slipped them on. Then I stepped outside and walked next door with Brian to the van that he and Natalie were using for hair and makeup. Inside, Naira was still in her purple flowered sundress, getting her makeup done. Cassandra was beside her, fully made-up and dressed in the red-and-yellow fish-pattern sarong, which Amanda had wrapped around her as a halter top. With it she wore a pair of slim white pants, red sandals, and the wooden bracelets that matched.

"Okay, Kerri," said Brian. He patted the empty chair in front of him. "Have a seat."

I sat down, and Brian began taking the rollers out of my hair.

"Cassandra," Naira said, closing her eyes so Natalie could brush some plum shadow across her eyelids, "I don't see why you don't just go look this stuff up at the library. There's one right here in South Beach, you know."

"I can't. I don't have *time*," Cassandra said. "I'm supposed to meet with him this afternoon. Please, just tell me everything you know about the place."

"I'm telling you, Cassandra, I don't know all that much more than you do," said Naira. "You could get more information from a guidebook."

She looked at Cassandra and sighed.

"Okay, here goes," said Naira. "The landmarked area is called the Art Deco District, and it stretches all along Ocean Drive. It's supposedly the biggest historic landmark area in the country, and it's one of the only ones with modern twentieth-century buildings in it...."

As Naira went on, I was surprised by how little I knew about South Beach, considering I had grown up only a few miles away. I guess if you live somewhere, there are a lot of things you never even learn about the place, but if you're a tourist you've got a reason to read guidebooks and stuff.

After Brian had taken out my rollers, he scrunched my new curls with his hands and then spritzed on hairspray to hold them. One thing about shooting in Florida is that it's humid, so your hair can get frizzy, even if it's straight.

"Okay, Kerri," said Brian. He patted me on the shoulder. "You're all done."

"Thanks, Bri," I said. I stood up and turned to Cassandra and Naira. "See you guys on the beach."

I walked out of the van and crossed Ocean Drive. Leslie had set up her camera on the strip of sand across from the promenade. Jackie and Alex were there talking to her. I walked over to Paige and Katerina, who were waiting nearby.

Paige's peach-and-white shell-design sarong was wrapped around her as a long skirt with a slit up the side. With it, she was wearing a cropped white top and white canvas shoes that laced around the ankles.

Katerina was wearing her blue-and-pink bird-pattern sarong as a halter dress. Her pale arms really stood out in the early morning light. It's a good thing it's so early, I thought, so none of us have to worry about getting too much sun. Katerina looked like she burned easily.

"Hey, you guys," I said.

"Hi, Kerri," said Paige.

"Hello. What is up?" said Katerina carefully.

I smiled.

"Not too much," I answered.

"Are you having fun being back in Miami?" asked Paige. "Or does it feel really strange to be back home?"

I thought a moment. "Well, probably a little of both," I said. "I mean, everything's still the same, I guess *I'm* just a little different now. But I saw my best friends from high school yesterday, and that was totally fun."

Paige shook her head. "I can't imagine what it would be like to go back to Nebraska for a shoot."

"I am thinking that my old friends would not understand what it is to be a model," said Katerina. "They are all dancers, so ballet is their life."

"I think some of my friends might be a little jealous," said Paige. "My little sister, Erin, would love watching a shoot, though. She's really into modeling. It's her idea of a dream come true."

I thought of my own sisters. I couldn't imagine either Andie or Casey ever wanting to model. They're each into their own things. Andie's the brain of the family. She's like Naira—her nose is always in a book and she won lots of awards when she was at Laurel Beach High. Casey's the artist. Ever since we were little, she could always draw and paint really well. Her idea of a dream come true would be getting accepted to the Miami Art Academy next fall.

"Hey," I said suddenly. "Speaking of dreams coming true, did you hear that Cassandra's got an appointment with Devon Redmond today?"

Paige sighed. "I know. She's so lucky she met him like that. If I ever walked into an elevator and saw Devon Redmond standing there, I'd be so nervous I'd fall apart."

"One time, I am remembering, in Russia, the great ballerina Alexandra Valyskova came to observe our class," said Katerina. "I was shaking so much I was losing my balance completely."

"Oh," I said. I guessed that was a pretty big deal to her.

Just then, Alex walked over to us, his walkie-talkie in his hand.

"Okay, you guys, the others are on their way over now," he said.

"Is Leslie ready for us?" I asked.

He nodded. "I think Jackie wants to do these as group shots to emphasize all the different ways the sarongs can be worn."

A few moments later, Cassandra, Naira, and Pia had arrived at the beach, along with Brian and Amanda. We were ready to go!

Leslie turned to Jackie. "How about having them all sit on that little wall there?" She pointed to the low seawall that separated the beach from the promenade.

Jackie nodded. "Let's try it. Okay, girls, let

me have you in this order, please—first Naira, then Pia, then Katerina, Kerri, Cassandra, and Paige."

"So," I said to Cassandra, as she took her place next to me on the wall, "did you get all the information you needed from Naira?"

She nodded. "I think. At least enough to get me through today's meeting." She shook her head. "That girl is like an encyclopedia."

"Excuse me, Jackie?" said Amanda. "I think we may have a problem putting Katerina next to Kerri like that, since the blues in their sarongs are so similar."

Jackie looked at us. "You're right. Kerri, switch with Paige, please."

Paige and I got up and exchanged places.

"Good," said Jackie. "That's much better."

"Hold on," said Leslie, looking through her camera. "I think everyone's going to have to move down a bit. I'm getting some of that volleyball net in the background."

I turned and saw a volleyball net set up in the sand just beyond us. The sight of it brought back all these memories. I *love* playing volleyball in the sand. I used to spend hours playing every summer on the beach near my house.

"Okay," said Jackie. "Let's have everyone move to the left a few yards."

We all got up and shifted further down on the seawall. Amanda made some adjustments to our sarongs, and we were ready to go. Leslie shot several rolls of us sitting there on the wall, and then paused, putting down her camera.

"You know, I think I'd like to see them in a little more of an action shot," she said.

"I agree with you," said Jackie.

Leslie looked around. "What do you say we go down to the water?" she suggested.

"Okay, let's give it a try," said Jackie.

We began to gather everything up. As we did, Katerina turned to me.

"Excuse me, please," she said. "May I ask you another question?"

"Shoot," I said.

She looked confused.

"It means 'Go ahead,'" I explained.

"Oh," she said. She nodded and frowned a little. "I am wondering, can you tell me please what is this little building for?" She pointed to one of the concession stands that lined the promenade.

"Oh, that's a fast-food stand," I said.

She looked confused again.

"Fast food?" I repeated. "You know, hamburgers, hot dogs, french fries."

"Ah, yes," she said. "This food is very American, is it not?"

"Yeah, I guess so," I said.

"Thank you," she said.

As we all headed down the beach toward the ocean, I saw Jackie and Leslie having a quick conference. I was pretty sure I knew what was coming next.

"Okay, girls, why don't you take off your shoes," said Leslie. "We're going to try having you wade through the waves a little."

"I knew it," I said to Cassandra. "What is it about the beach that makes photographers want to stick you in the water? I bet half the shoots I did when I was down here with Sunshine involved wet feet."

"I know," said Cass. She bent down to unstrap her sandals. "It was like that in Rio, too."

I didn't mind, though. I was actually looking forward to putting my feet in the cool, salty water. I've always loved the ocean, and I'd been so busy since I'd gotten to South Beach that I hadn't had time to go in for a dip yet.

Jackie still wanted all of us to be in the same shot, so Leslie had us line up in a row and put our arms around each other's shoulders and waists. Then she asked us all to walk along the beach together with our feet in the water.

Since I was at the end of the row, I ended up being in less water than anyone else. My ankles didn't even get wet. But just feeling that little bit of water made me determined to go for a swim soon.

Meanwhile, Naira, who was on the other end of the line, was in water up to her knees. Between the splashing we all made by walking together and the crashing of the waves, she ended up being soaked all the way to her waist. Her turquoise-and-white flowered sarong, which had been tied as a strapless minidress, was drenched. Naira's a good sport about stuff like that, though. She's been modeling since she was little, and she's got a very professional attitude.

Finally, we were finished. We all trudged back across the sand toward the promenade.

"So," I said to Cassandra, "what time's your big meeting this afternoon?"

"Two o'clock," she answered, her eyes

sparkling with excitement at the thought. "I'm supposed to meet him in the lobby. Hey, I have an idea, Kerri! Why don't you just *happen* to walk through on your way to your room or something? Then I can introduce you."

"I wish I could," I said. "But I'm scheduled for a shoot at one-thirty."

"Oh, *que mal,* what a pain," she said. "One-thirty, that's a hot time of day for a shoot."

"It's indoors," I told her. "At the South Beach Studios, just a couple of blocks from here, right on Ocean Drive."

"Oh," she said. "Well, that's good."

We made our way toward the promenade. I could see that it was already filling up with people strolling, jogging, Rollerblading, skateboarding, and riding bicycles. I really love how in Florida you can exercise outside practically anytime you want. It's always warm, and even when it rains, the showers blow over pretty quickly.

I remembered the way Heather always suggested having cheerleading practice outside by the football field. We pretended that we did it because it was better to practice by the field, where we would actually be cheering. But we all knew it was mainly so we could watch the guys on the team work out.

Thinking of the football team made me think of Steve Bishop. I couldn't believe that Heather was going out with him now. I remembered her making jokes about him the year before because he used to eat alone in the cafeteria a lot. It made me realize that one of the reasons I'd never told my friends that I thought he was cute was because he was such a loner. I guess I'd been afraid he might not really fit in with our crowd.

But if he was going out with Heather, that meant he was part of our crowd now. I thought of the party at the Jenkinses' later that night. Steve would probably be there with Heather. That was going to be totally weird. Then I had an idea.

"Hey, Cass," I said. "How'd you like to go to a party tonight in Laurel Beach? It should be lots of fun. All my old friends are going to be there, and you could meet them."

"I don't think I can, Kerri," she said. "I'm scheduled for a sunset shoot on some little island near here. It could run late. Besides, I'm trying to leave as much of my time free as possible in case I get Devon Redmond to agree to tape an interview. Sorry."

"It's okay," I said. "I understand."

"Hey," she said, "what do you say we grab some lunch before your shoot? I saw a great little café about a block from the hotel. It looks perfect for checking out the local scenery, if you know what I mean."

"Sure," I said, laughing. As usual, I knew exactly what she meant.

CHAPTER 9

"Okay, girls, that's it," said Leslie. She put down her camera and started to rewind the film. "You can all go now."

"Beautiful work, you three," said Jackie.

It was four in the afternoon. Pia, Naira, and I had just finished the shoot at South Beach Studios. We'd been posing in brightly colored minidresses—another *Style* forecast for summer—holding bunches of daisies.

I walked carefully off the piece of turquoise seamless that had been rolled down onto the floor as a backdrop, and I put my daisies on a table.

"Thanks, Kerri," said Jackie.

Pia, Naira, and I headed into the dressing room together.

"*Che giorno!* What a day!" sighed Pia. She started unbuttoning the front of her bright

99

green minidress. "I am tired."

"Yeah, me too," I said. I pulled my magenta minidress over my head.

"I am glad there is not more work tonight," said Pia. She stepped into her own long flowered skirt.

"You're lucky," said Naira. "*I* have a shoot tonight."

"Oh, you mean that one on the island?" I asked, remembering what Cass had told me.

Naira nodded.

"I do not understand," said Pia. "How do you stay so energetic, Naira?"

"I just make sure to get plenty of rest," Naira answered. "Believe me, I learned that the hard way."

Naira let herself get totally overworked and exhausted a little while ago. She ended up getting really sick.

Naira turned her back toward me. "Can you undo me, Kerri?"

"Sure," I said.

I unzipped the bright yellow minidress she was wearing, which was the one that hadn't worked on Pia at the fitting in New York. Naira put on her own sundress, and I changed back into my own gray tank top and black bicycle shorts. We walked outside into the bright sunlight.

Ocean Drive was crowded with people, strolling among the cafés. Across the street was the winding pink promenade. Beyond the promenade was the beach, where people were playing Frisbee and brightly colored umbrellas ruffled in the breeze.

"Hey, you guys, want to walk back to the hotel along the beach?" I asked.

"Thanks anyway, but I'm hungry," said Naira. "I'm going to grab something to eat at one of these cafés here."

"I will walk that way with you, Kerri," said Pia.

"Okay," I said. "Great. Catch you later, Ni."

"Bye," she said.

Pia and I crossed the promenade. At the seawall, we bent over and took off our shoes.

"Mmmm, the sea air is *molto rinfrescante,* very refreshing, to breathe, don't you think?" said Pia. She stuffed her sandals into her bag.

"The best," I agreed. I tied my laces together and slung my sneakers over my shoulder.

"When I was a child, I used to visit my grandparents at the seaside every summer," Pia said wistfully as we walked through the sand. "They lived in Amalfi, a section of Italy that is *molto bello,* very beautiful."

"You don't go there anymore?" I asked her.

"Ah, *magari,* I wish," she said. "But my grandmother has died and my grandfather has moved to Rome to live with my family." She shook her head. "Of course, Rome is a very beautiful city, too. But I miss my visits to Amalfi very much."

"Yeah, I know how that is," I said. "I grew up here, near the beach. I love living in New York, but sometimes I miss feeling the sand between my toes."

We were getting close to the section of the beach where Leslie had shot us in the sarongs that morning. I could see the volleyball net nearby. A few people had gathered there. A tall, blond guy in a striped bathing suit was tossing a volleyball up in the air.

I nodded toward the net. "That's another thing I miss," I said. "Do people play volleyball on the beach in Italy?"

Pia shook her head. "No, not really. On the beach, and everywhere in Italy, it is *calcio. Calcio* is this game you call soccer." She rolled her eyes. "*Calcio, calcio, calcio!* My brothers speak of almost nothing else. They are, how you say, *appassionati*, big fans."

"Beach volleyball's the best," I told her. Then I had an idea. "Hey, come on. It looks like they might be starting a game. I'll show you how to play."

"Ah, no, *grazie*, thank you, anyway," she said.

"Oh, come on, Pia," I said. "It's totally fun. You'll see."

She shook her head. "*Mi dispiace*, I'm sorry, but I am not dressed for playing," she said, looking down at her long skirt. "Besides, I am too tired. Now I wish only to return to the hotel and relax with the air-conditioning. But you go ahead and play."

I looked over at the net. The blond guy had started a volley with a girl in a blue tank suit. It looked like they were about to start a game.

I was tired from working, but a game of beach volleyball would be fun. Besides, I hadn't had as much time for exercise as I would have liked since we had arrived in South Beach. It would be a good workout for me.

"Okay, I think I will play," I said. I grabbed my bag and took out the tube of sunscreen I always carry with me. "Do me a favor, Pia," I said as I rubbed some on my arms. "Leave a message for Alex at the hotel saying I decided to hang out at the beach for a while, okay?"

"*Certo,* of course, Kerri," she said. "Enjoy the game!"

I finished applying the sunscreen and trotted across the sand toward the group by the net.

"Hey," I called to the guy in the striped suit. "Are you guys playing?"

"Sure," he called back. "Are you in?"

"Yeah," I said. He popped me the ball and I hit it back to him.

As we tapped the ball back and forth, warming up, the group around us grew bigger. Soon we had a big enough crowd for a game.

It was great to be playing again. I gave it my all, sinking down on my knees and even diving into the sand to make the tough shots. When I'm into a physical activity, it's easy for me to forget about everything else that's going on around me. It wasn't until the end of the third game that I realized I was totally sweaty, covered with sand, and exhausted.

I tossed the ball to the blond guy.

"Giving up so soon?" he asked with a grin.

"I have to," I panted.

I waved and headed toward the ocean. I wished I had my bathing suit on. A dip would feel great right about now. Well, at least I could wade in a little bit.

I dropped my bag in the sand and walked into the ocean. I could almost feel my hot feet sizzling as they hit the cool water. I walked in up to my thighs and splashed a little water on my face.

Just then, a Jet Ski roared by, creating a huge wave. Before I could back up, the wave crashed over me, drenching me from the chest down. I looked down at my wet tank top and bicycle shorts. Oh, well, I thought, I might as well go in now. So I dove in and swam down the beach a bit and back. It felt great.

As I walked out of the ocean, I heard a familiar voice.

"Is this some kind of native Florida girl thing, swimming in your clothes?"

I wiped the water from my eyes and saw Claude, from the night before, standing on the sand nearby. He was wearing a baggy black bathing suit and round sunglasses.

"Hi," I said. I wrung the water out of my

hair. "I was really hot and I didn't have my suit with me."

"So," he said, "what happened to you last night? One minute you were there talking to me and the next minute you were gone."

"Sorry about that," I said. "I had to find a friend." I picked up my bag. "Besides, it looked like you and Pia were having a pretty nice conversation."

He looked at me. "I wanted to be having a nice conversation with you."

"Oh," I said. I didn't know what to say. Claude was nice, but I didn't like him the way he seemed to like me.

"Well, maybe we can have that conversation another time," he said, looking at me. "How about tonight?"

"Tonight?" I said.

I thought a moment. I *could* invite him to the Jenkinses' party, but I couldn't see Claude, in his cool city clothes and slicked-back hair, fitting in very well with the gang from Laurel Beach. Besides, I only liked him as a friend, so it might not be fair to him. He might think of it as a date or something.

"Um, sorry," I said. "I'm busy tonight. But maybe another time."

"Sure," he said. "I'll give you a call. You're at the Fairleigh, right?"

"Yeah," I said.

The Fairleigh. I realized how exhausted I really was. I wished I was back at the Fairleigh this very minute. It had been a long day, and I'd been up since dawn. The volleyball game and the swim had just about done me in.

I looked toward Ocean Drive, and spotted the hotel's pink-and-yellow facade. It was just over the promenade and across the street—not very far at all—but it seemed about a million miles away.

Back in my room at the Fairleigh, I took off my wet clothes and put on an old T-shirt of my dad's. Then I sat down on my bed to look at the little pink message slips that had been waiting for me at the front desk.

2:15 p.m.—*Your mother called.*
3:05 p.m.—*Call Heather about party tonight.*
4:15 p.m.—*Sloane called. Wants to know if you can come to dinner at your father's.*

I sighed. I knew I should really call everyone back. But I was *so* tired. Maybe if I just lay down for a moment first...

The sound of a door closing woke me up. I opened my eyes, but everything was still dark. Then a light went on.

"Oh!" said Katerina. "I am sorry, Kerri. I did not realize that you were sleeping."

"No, no, that's okay," I said. I sat up on the bed, yawned, and rubbed my eyes. I looked out the window and was shocked to see that it was dark out. "What time is it?"

Katerina looked at her watch. "Almost nine o'clock," she said.

"Nine?" I repeated. I'd been asleep for over three hours! "Oh my gosh, I'd better call Heath," I said.

"Excuse me?" said Katerina.

"Nothing," I said. "I just have to make a phone call."

I reached for the phone by the bed, lay back down, and dialed Heather's number. The phone rang and rang. Katerina lay down on her bed and opened up her *Jody & Jimmy* comic book.

Finally, Heather's father answered the phone sounding out of breath. "Hello?"

"Hi, Mr. Burke, it's Kerri," I said. "Is Heather there?"

"No, she isn't," he said. "I believe she went out with some friends for the evening."

"Oh," I said. I guessed she must be at the Jenkinses' already. "Well, thanks."

"Any message?" he asked.

"No," I said. "That's okay. Bye."

Next I tried Jess. But she wasn't home, either. They must have gone to the party. I thought about trying them over there. After all, the Jenkinses were probably listed. Maybe I could get someone to come over and pick me up. But the more I thought about it, the more I realized that I didn't really feel that much like getting up and getting dressed, anyway. It felt so good to lie down. Besides, I was scheduled for an early shoot the next morning. And I'd be seeing Heather and Jessa at the game the next day. It would probably be a good idea to just stay in and get some rest.

I hung up the phone and turned to Katerina.

"Where is everyone?" I asked.

She put down her comic book. "In the restaurant," she said, "eating dinner."

"Mmm," I said. "Dinner." I *was* kind of

hungry. But going downstairs would mean getting up and getting dressed. Then I had an idea.

"Hey, Katerina," I said. "I think I'm going to order room service. Do you want something?"

She looked at me. "Room service?" she repeated.

"Yeah," I said. "You know, food that they bring up to the room."

Katerina grimaced. "Oh, food," she said. "No, I don't think so." She put her hand to her stomach.

"Are you all right?" I asked.

"*Da*, I mean, yes, I think I will be," she said. She made another face. "It is just that I had a little too much American food today."

"American food?" I said. "What do you mean?"

She looked at me. "But Kerri, you were the one who told me about this food," she said. "What did you call it? Food-in-a-hurry? Speedy food? Quick food?"

Then I realized what she was referring to. "Oh!" I said. I tried not to laugh. "You mean *fast* food."

"Yes, yes," she said. She waved her hand

feebly. "That is it. But I am afraid I may have eaten it a little *too* fast, because my stomach pains me."

"What exactly did you have?" I asked her.

She began to count on her fingers. "Hamburger, hot dog, french fries, ice cream—"

I cut her off. "You ate all that?"

She nodded. "I was very anxious to try all American fast foods," she said.

This time I couldn't hold it in. The whole thing was *so* funny. I started to laugh out loud.

At first Katerina looked a little hurt, and then, suddenly, she started laughing, too. The sight of her laughing just made me laugh harder. Soon we were both clutching our sides.

"Oh, Katerina," I said. I wiped away a tear. "You shouldn't have done that! Do you know how disgustingly greasy all that stuff is?"

She laughed even harder. "I am sorry to say, yes, I do know now!" she said. She took a deep breath and let it out with a sigh. "It is only that I am so excited to learn as quickly as I can everything about this country," she went on. "And there is so much to learn. In the language, for instance. There is much that is not

111

taught in my English books. Like the meaning of 'What's up?,' and about the nicknames."

"Yeah," I said. "I guess they wouldn't teach that kind of stuff in books, would they?"

She shook her head. "And for me, it is these lessons that are most important. So I am trying to learn what I can from the television and from reading these comic books." She held up her *Jody & Jimmy* comic.

"*Oh*," I said. That explained a lot.

"But it is sometimes very difficult," she said. She lowered her voice. "This is why I envy you."

"Me?" I said. "You envy me?"

"Yes," she said. She looked at me. "All that I am working so hard to learn, it comes very easily to you. What do you say? Easy as cake."

"Pie," I corrected. "Easy as pie."

She sighed. "You see?" she said. "I still have much to learn. But you, you already know it all, Kerri. You are average American teenager."

I smiled. Normally, I wouldn't have appreciated being called average. But knowing what Katerina thought of the average American teenager, I took it as a compliment.

"I guess I see what you mean," I said. "I do lead a pretty typical American teenager's life. I mean, I did. Not so much anymore, though."

Katerina sighed. "This is what I am wishing to experience."

I smiled. "Let me give you a little advice," I said. "Next time, don't try to experience all that greasy food at once." I picked up the room service menu from the night table. "Now, I am going to order myself some dinner, and I'm going to get you exactly what any typical American teenager would have for a stomachache like that: a nice, bubbly American ginger ale."

CHAPTER 10

"Okay, girls," Leslie called from behind her camera. It was Saturday morning. "Take a step or two to your left, closer to the building."

Leslie was shooting Cassandra and me on Ocean Drive, in front of this really pretty hotel, the Caron, not too far from the Fairleigh. The two of us moved in unison, edging closer to the outside wall of the pink-and-pale-blue building.

We were both wearing long, thin, sheer cotton dresses with pretty, lacy slips underneath. Cassandra's dress was white, and mine was very pale yellow. Amanda had given us little white crocheted caps and white ballet slippers.

"You know," said Cassandra, nodding toward the Caron, "back when most of these hotels were built, over fifty years ago, this was considered a very chic place to vacation."

"That's nice, girls," said Leslie. The camera clicked. "Just act like you're having a casual conversation."

We *are* having a casual conversation, I thought to myself. Cassandra and I had been having the same casual conversation all morning. Her meeting with Devon Redmond had gone great the day before. He had even agreed to do an interview with her for *Qual o lance?* on Sunday. Now she couldn't stop telling everyone facts about South Beach and Art Deco architecture.

"That's right," she continued. "*Everybody* who was *anybody* came to South Beach back then. It was very glamorous."

"That's what it's like now," I pointed out.

"Sure," said Cassandra, "but it wasn't always that way. There was some time in between when the whole area was terribly run-down."

"Hold on a second," said Brian. "Kerri's got a stray hair." He walked over and ran a comb through my low ponytail which fell across one shoulder. "Okay, fine."

Leslie resumed her shooting.

"In fact," Cassandra went on, "things were falling apart *so* much that they came close to just tearing down all these buildings and putting up some big convention center or something."

"Really?" I said. I hadn't known that, either. It was weird to try to imagine this area without all the candy-colored hotels.

"That's right," said Cassandra. "That's when the organization Devon's with stepped in."

"*Devon?*" I asked, raising my eyebrows. "Hmm, sounds like you two are getting pretty chummy, Cass."

She flashed me a grin. "Did I tell you he's taking me on a walking tour of the area this afternoon?"

"Only about fifty times," I said, grinning back.

"Okay, girls, not so smiley," said Leslie.

"Yes," said Jackie. "These are very demure dresses. The big smiles don't look right with them."

I relaxed my face.

"Have you figured out how you're going to do the interview on Sunday?" I asked Cassandra. "I mean, how you're going to get yourself on camera, too?"

"No," said Cassandra. She frowned. "I thought of asking someone else to film it, but I know Roberto's really into this 'girl with a camera' thing."

"Cassandra, don't scowl so much," called Jackie. "We don't want you to grin, but the scowl doesn't look right either."

"I'd better stop thinking about that," said Cassandra to me with a sigh. "If I keep it up I'll ruin all the shots."

Half an hour later, we were done. Cassandra and I headed back to the hotel room. When we got there, Katerina was gone. Cassandra sat down to give herself a manicure, and I picked up the phone to call Heather.

Her brother, Jake, answered the phone. "Hello?"

"Hi, Jake," I said. "It's me, Kerri. Is Heath around?"

"Hey, Kerri," he said. "Yeah, she's just getting out of the pool. Hang on a sec. Heather, it's for you!"

I heard Heather pick up the cordless by the pool. "Hello?"

"Hi, Heath, it's me," I said.

She was silent for a moment.

"Kerri," she said then. "I was wondering when you'd call."

"Actually, I called last night," I said. "But I guess you were already at the party."

"You called?" she said. "That's funny. No one gave me a message."

"Well, I didn't leave a message," I said. "I realized that you'd already left, and I was pretty tired anyway."

"Why didn't you call earlier?" she asked. "Jessa and I thought you were coming to the party with us, you know."

"Yeah, I'm sorry about that, " I said. "I overslept. I've had a pretty busy work schedule since I've been down here. But I'm free now."

She didn't say anything.

"Hey, Heather," I said. "What's up? Are you mad at me or something?"

She sighed. "No, not really, Kerri. Just disappointed, I guess. I mean, we were all *really* looking forward to seeing you last night. And then we didn't even *hear* from you—"

"I know, I'm sorry, really," I said.

"The thing is, when you first called and

said you were coming down here to visit, we all got really excited," she said. "We thought it was going to be the three of us, just like old times. But we've only seen you once since you got here, at Pop's, and that was only for a little bit."

"Look," I said, "I'm sorry, but I told you I've been really busy working. Right now I'm completely free for the rest of the day." I paused. "And I'm getting a super-strong craving to see a Laurel Lions game."

Heather laughed. "Having you at a game will be just like old times, Kerri. We can't put you back on the squad, but I bet we can get you a seat right behind the cheerleaders' bench. I'll drive down and pick you up right now, okay?"

"Sure thing, Heath," I said. "See ya in a few."

The moment I hung up the phone, it rang again. I had a feeling I knew who it was. I hadn't called my mother back yet, but I'd just been so busy.

I answered the phone. "Hi, Mom."

"Uh, Kerri?" said a male voice on the other end of the line.

"Yes?" I said. I was totally embarrassed.

"This is Claude."

"Oh, Claude, hi," I said. "Sorry, I thought you were my mother."

"Boy, she must have a pretty deep voice," he joked.

I laughed.

"Listen," he said. "How about letting me take you up on that rain check you gave me yesterday? I thought maybe we could go out to lunch."

"I can't," I said. "I've just made plans."

"Well, then, how about dinner?"

I thought a moment. I might be back from the game in time for dinner. And I guessed it wouldn't hurt to go out with him once. Then again, dinner with Claude might go late. I *was* scheduled for a shoot at five o'clock the next morning.

"I really don't think I can," I said. "But thanks anyway, Claude."

"Okay, sure, Kerri," he said. He sounded disappointed.

After I got off the phone, I called Alex's room and left him a message, telling him where I was going. I had planned on giving my mother a call after that, but the moment I hung up the phone it rang again. This time it was the front desk downstairs, letting me know that Heather had arrived and was waiting with her car. I'd just have to try my mom later, when I got back.

> "We've got the guys in the Lions' green,
> They're a great big fighting machine!
> Green is for go, and they won't stop,
> They're gonna take it to the TOP!
> GO-O-O-O-O TEAM!!!"

I sat behind the cheerleaders and watched as Heather, Jessa, and the rest of the squad waved their green-and-white pom-poms. It was weird to be sitting in the bleachers instead of being out there on the field, cheering with them. I knew every single cheer—except one, which must have been new this year—and I mouthed the words along with them.

Still, one nice thing about sitting in the bleachers was that I got to see what was going on on the field. When you're cheering, you're so busy you barely even get a chance to watch the game.

And what a game it was! For a while there, things didn't look too good for the Lions. The game was almost over and they were down, 9–3. Then, with two seconds on the clock,

Steve Bishop caught a pass for a touchdown. The Laurel Lions got the extra point and beat the Freshwater Gators, 10–9.

The crowd went crazy. Everyone jumped up screaming. People were hugging each other and high-fiving. The cheerleaders threw their pom-poms up in the air, and the football players crushed Steve in a huge group bear hug. I hurried down to the field.

"Hey!" said Jessa when she saw me. "Some game you picked to come back for, eh, Kerri?"

"The best," I agreed. "And you guys looked totally fantastic."

Heather turned to me. Her cheeks were flushed and her face was slightly damp. "Did you like the new cheer?"

"It was great," I told her. "Was that yours?"

She nodded. "It just came to me, right in the middle of English class."

She picked her pom-poms up off the ground.

"You're coming to the barbecue, aren't you, Kerri?" she asked.

"Barbecue?" I said.

"Oh yeah," said Jessa. "I guess we forgot to tell you. There's a big barbecue now, over at the Bear's house."

"The Bear" was Bob Berkowsky, the Lions' wide receiver. He was huge, about six feet tall and two hundred pounds, with a really wild sense of humor.

"Come, Kerri," said Heather. "It'll be fun."

I looked at my watch. Five–fifteen. I had plenty of time to go with them to the barbecue and still get back to the hotel in time to get a good night's sleep.

"Okay, sure, great," I said.

A barbecue at the Bear's house was bound to be tons of fun. Everybody from the game would be there. It would be just like old times.

Just then, Steve Bishop came trotting over to where we were standing. He had his green helmet in his hand, and his dark curls were plastered down on his forehead. He was cuter than ever.

He threw one arm around Heather's shoulders and gave her a kiss.

"Hey," he said, looking at me, "Kerri, right? How's it going?"

"Great," I said, suddenly finding myself grinning like an idiot and nodding my head up and down. "Really great game, Steve."

"Thanks," he said, planting another kiss on

the top of Heather's head. "You coming to the barbecue?"

"Sure," I said, still nodding. "You bet."

"Kerri, are you all right?" asked Jessa. "You look kind of funny."

"Yeah," I said. I watched as Heather and Steve strolled away with their arms around each other. "I'm fine."

But I'd just had a thought. A thought that made me feel funny inside. And this was it—what if I hadn't gone to New York to model for Ford? What if Nancy Lloyd had never discovered me that day on the beach? Could that have been me strolling toward the parking lot in my cheerleader's uniform with Steve, instead of Heather?

CHAPTER 11

"Hey, Heath," I said, "can I talk to you a second?"

"Just a minute," she said. She was balancing two paper plates with hamburgers on them and a plastic cup of soda in her hands. "Let me just take this stuff over to Steve."

She made her way across the lawn and into a crowd of people. I looked at my watch and sighed. It was after nine o'clock, and we were *still* at the barbecue. I'd forgotten how long these after-game parties could go on, especially when the Lions had won.

When ten minutes had gone by and Heather hadn't come back, I went to look for her. I made my way through the crowd and by the barbecue grill with its sizzling burgers and dogs. The grill made me think of Katerina. I supposed this "typical American" barbecue would be her idea of heaven.

Personally, I was a little tired of being there. Sure, it was fun at first, but as time went on I started to worry about getting back to the hotel in time to get a good night's sleep. A five o'clock shoot meant getting up at four, even earlier if I wanted to get in my sit-ups. If I went to bed right away I could barely get seven hours of sleep.

But I couldn't go to bed if I couldn't find Heather to drive me back to the Fairleigh. Just then, I saw Jessa talking to Heidi Gourney, one of the girls who had been on the swim team with me. I walked over to them.

"Hi, Kerri," said Heidi when she saw me.

"Hi," I said. "How's the swim team doing this year?"

"Oh, pretty good," she said. "How's life in New York?"

"Really fun," I told her.

"Gosh," she said. "It must be so great living up there and modeling like that. What an incredibly cool life."

Try getting up at four o'clock tomorrow morning and tell me how cool you feel, I wanted to say. But instead I said, "It's fun."

I turned to Jessa. "Have you seen Heather? I think I need to get back to the hotel pretty soon."

"But it's so early!" said Jessa.

"Yeah, well, I have to work really early in the morning."

"Work?" said Heidi, confused. "You have a job here? I thought you were just visiting."

"I'm down here on a job," I explained. "For *Style* magazine."

"Oh," said Heidi. "Modeling. When you said work, I thought you meant...you know, *work.*"

Modeling *is* work, I thought to myself. But I guessed I couldn't expect Heidi to understand. After all, if you've never done it, modeling does seem like it's mostly fun and glamour.

"Well, I guess I'd better go look for Heather," I said.

"Okay, Kerri," said Jessa. "Catch you later."

I finally found Heather twenty minutes later. She and Steve were sitting on a little bench-swing at the side of the house, holding hands. I got the feeling that I'd interrupted a romantic moment. But right then, I didn't care. It was a quarter to ten, and I really had to get back to the hotel.

"Heath," I said, "I've been looking all over the place for you."

"Oh, hi, Kerri," she said. She leaned closer to Steve.

"Hi," said Steve with a big grin.

"Listen, Heath," I said. "I *really* need to get back to South Beach."

"Okay, sure," she said. "In a little while, okay, Ker?"

"Well, actually, I kind of need to go right away," I said.

She turned to Steve. "Just a sec, Steve, okay?" She walked over to where I was standing. "Kerri," she said in a low voice, "can't you wait just a *little* bit longer?"

I shook my head. "I really have to go now," I said.

"But it's not even ten o'clock yet," she said.

"I know," I said. "But that's late for me. You see, I have a really early shoot tomorrow morning."

"Oh, come on," she said. "You can stay a little longer, can't you?" She glanced back at Steve. "*Please?*"

I hesitated. I knew how much it meant to Heather to stay at the party with Steve. But I also knew how important it was for me to get a good night's sleep.

Heather turned back toward Steve. "I'll take you in a little while, Kerri, I promise," she said over her shoulder. "Okay?"

But it wasn't okay. From the way things looked, Heather could be there a long time with Steve. Now I knew that I never should have agreed to come to the barbecue in the first place. It wasn't like going somewhere with Cassandra, who would understand that I wanted to look my best the next day. It was pretty clear that my Laurel Beach friends weren't really taking my modeling obligations that seriously.

I wondered what I should do. I guessed I could call my mother and ask her to come pick me up and take me back to South Beach. Somehow it just didn't seem right, though, since I hadn't made time to see her yet or even returned her latest phone call.

Then I knew what to do. In New York, if I was ever stuck somewhere or couldn't figure out how to get back to the apartment by myself, I would just step out into the street and hail a yellow cab. I knew Laurel Beach had a cab company, because I'd seen the navy blue radio cars driving around sometimes. I'd just call myself a taxi.

By the time the taxi dropped me off at the Fairleigh, it was quarter after ten. Katerina and Cassandra were both asleep, so I undressed as quickly as I could in the dark and climbed into bed.

I expected to fall asleep as soon as my head hit the pillow, but for some reason, I just couldn't seem to get comfortable. I tossed and turned for what seemed like hours. Images kept running through my head—the game, the party, Heather and Steve. And I kept thinking about what Heidi had said, and how she seemed to think that modeling was all glamour and not a serious job. Thinking about it was making me really mad, and it takes a lot to get me angry.

What was really bugging me was the fact that my old friends seemed like they didn't really understand my new life at all. But I was also beginning to wonder if having my new life was worth giving up being, as Katerina would say, "an average American teenager."

Then I heard a funny sound, like a whimper. I rolled over. Cassandra was still sleeping heavily, her breath deep and regular. I looked at Katerina. I could just make her out in the lavender glow of the neon trim outside the window. She was lying on her side, facing away from me, with the sheet pulled up over her neck. Beneath the blanket, I could see her shoulders shaking. I heard another funny little sound, and I realized that she was crying!

"Katerina?" I said softy. "Katerina, are you okay?"

Her answer was muffled by the blankets.

"Kat?" I said again. "I can't hear you. Is something wrong?"

She moaned softly. "I do not think I can move," she said.

Quickly, I got out of bed and hurried over to her. She was still on her side, and I could see tears glistening on her cheeks.

"What is it?" I asked her. "Are you hurt?"

"It is my back," she said. "I think it has received too much sun."

"Oh," I said. "You mean you got a sunburn. Let me take a look." I switched on the light by her bed.

She pulled down the sheet and gingerly

lifted the back of her white cotton pajama top. When I saw her back, I gasped. It was bright red. I put my hand on it and she winced. It was hot to the touch.

"What is up, Kerri?" she managed to say.

I shook my head. "You got it bad, Kat. *Really* bad. How did you let this happen?"

"It was accident," she said. "I was lying on a towel observing the American beach life. Then I fell asleep."

I nodded to myself. The Florida sun was super strong and Katerina had such fair skin. It wouldn't have taken long for her to get burnt.

"Maybe I should go tell Jackie," I suggested.

"No!" Katerina pleaded. "Please do not speak to Jackie."

"But Kat," I said, "this could be really serious."

"Please," she said again. She began to cry. "If Jackie discovers this, she will cancel me from the shoot tomorrow morning, and I will be in trouble."

"All right," I said, "I won't tell."

Just then, Cassandra rolled over in her bed.

"Could you guys keep it down?" she mumbled. "I'm trying to get some sleep."

"Cass," I said. "Cass, wake up."

"What?" she said. She turned her head and squinted at me. "Is it morning already?"

"No," I said, "but I need your help with something. Katerina's got a sunburn."

"She'll feel better in the morning," said Cassandra. She rolled over and put the sheet over her head.

"No, really, Cass," I said. "It's bad."

Cassandra sighed and got out of bed. "All right," she said. "Show me."

"There," I said, pointing to Katerina's back.

"*Puxa!* Wow!" said Cassandra. "That looks terrible."

"Also it feels terrible," said Katerina.

"I've got just the thing for that," said Cassandra. She walked over to her night table and opened her cosmetic kit. She took out a tube of cream. "Here, this is mentholated. It won't make the burn go away but it will help you feel a little better."

Cassandra and I put the cream on Katerina's back. It must have hurt a whole lot because tears welled up in her eyes again.

When we finished, Katerina sat up on the edge of her bed and tried to smile. "This is feeling a little better, I think," she said.

Cassandra shook her head. "It's going to hurt you for at least a couple of days, though."

"She's scheduled for tomorrow morning's shoot," I said.

"Well, I don't think Jackie will think you should be in the pictures when she sees *this*," said Cassandra.

Katerina's lower lip began to tremble.

"I told her we wouldn't tell Jackie," I said. "She's afraid she might get in trouble." I thought a moment. "What are we supposed to wear tomorrow, do you know?"

"Probably the evening gowns," said Cassandra. "Tomorrow's my last shoot, and that's the only thing I tried on at the fitting that I haven't worn yet."

Katerina nodded. "It is the same with me."

"Which gown did you try at the fitting?" I asked Katerina.

"The gold," she said. "With the little jacket attached."

"Perfect," I said. "It doesn't show your back at all, right?"

"That is correct," said Katerina.

Cassandra winced. "Yeah, but that gold material is so scratchy. It's going to kill your back."

"She's right," I said to Katerina. "Are you sure you can handle it?"

Katerina straightened her back and put her chin in the air.

"I will have to," she said.

CHAPTER 12

"All right, Katerina, have a seat right here," Brian said early the following morning. He patted the chair in front of him.

Cassandra and I exchanged a quick look as Katerina lowered herself into the chair. She was very careful to keep her back from touching it. The three of us, along with Naira, Paige, and Pia, were at the Palm Club, a fancy luxury hotel in downtown Miami. Jackie had arranged to use the Palm Club's glass-enclosed, rooftop swimming pool area for the evening-gown shoot. Amanda, Natalie, and Brian had turned the pool's dressing areas into makeshift hair, makeup, and dressing rooms.

Naira, Paige, and Pia had already been made-up and had their hair done. Now they were in the dressing room with Amanda, changing into their gowns.

Natalie finished Katerina's makeup and Brian started on her hair.

I'd kept my eye on Katerina since we'd arrived. She was managing but she definitely looked uncomfortable. The white T-shirt she was wearing under her sundress hid her burned back completely. She was moving pretty stiffly, though, and she had an uncomfortable look on her face. I wondered if she was going to be okay. Especially once she changed into that scratchy gold gown.

Meanwhile, I was having problems of my own. I guess working all weekend and seeing my friends had finally caught up with me. Plus the hours I had spent tossing and turning the night before hadn't helped. By the time we'd finished with Katerina, it had been two in the morning, which meant I'd had only two hours of sleep.

Unfortunately, I'm not one of those people who can stay awake all night and look perky the next day. Instead, it really shows if I don't get at least eight hours of sleep. When I'm overtired, my face has this way of getting puffy and I get big dark circles under my eyes.

It turned out that I wasn't the only one who noticed them, either. As soon as I sat down in the makeup chair, Natalie clucked her tongue at me.

"Boy," she said, "look at you. Late night?"

"Kind of," I said. "Can you do anything about it?"

She pursed her lips.

"Let's try an ice-water bath," she said. "That will help reduce the puffiness."

She picked up a plastic bowl from a table nearby.

"Alex?" she called. "Do me a favor and go find an ice machine somewhere, would you?"

Ten minutes later, I held my breath and plunged my face into the bowl of ice water.

"Now, just stay there as long as you can stand it," I heard Natalie instructing me from above.

No problem, I thought. I can hold my breath for a long time. I guess it's from swimming. Natalie must have started to get worried though, because she tapped me on the shoulder.

"Kerri," she said. "You okay? Don't fall asleep in there, kid."

I lifted my face out of the water, and she handed me a towel to pat it dry.

"Wow," I said, "that feels much better." I felt a lot more awake, too.

"And you look a little better as well," she said. She peered at me. "Let's see what we can do to cover up those dark circles."

After Natalie finished my makeup, Brian did my hair. Since we were shooting evening gowns, Jackie wanted the hair to be sort of formal-looking, too. So Brian pulled my hair up and arranged it in a fluffy pile on top of my head.

"I don't know about this hairstyle Brian gave me, Cass," I said, as the three of us went to the dressing room to get our gowns from Amanda. "I feel like I have a soft-serve ice cream cone on top of my head."

Cassandra laughed. "It doesn't look that way, believe me, Kerri," she said. "It's very elegant."

I shrugged. I trust Cassandra's taste, but I'm not as used to dressing up as she is. Cass grew up around evening gowns and fancy parties. Her parents live in this elegant penthouse in Brazil, and they're always going out to balls and stuff. Her mother even has her own dressmaker.

We walked into the dressing room, passing Paige, Naira, and Pia on their way out. Paige was wearing the gorgeous cream-colored Rudolfo gown she had tried on in New York. Her red hair was in a French twist, and she had on little dangling crystal earrings.

Naira had on a pretty pink gown that looked like something Cinderella would have worn. The sleeves were off-the-shoulder and trimmed with little pink silk rosebuds, and the skirt was really full. Little pearls had been threaded through her hair which was pulled back in a bun.

Pia was wearing a long, sleeveless black gown, with a little mock turtleneck. A black satin bow was tied in her hair as a headband.

When we got into the dressing room, Amanda gave us our gowns. Mine was the deep purple one with the slit up the side that I had tried on in New York for her, the one that had been taken in at the waist. Amanda handed Cassandra a strapless white gown with a sequined bodice. Then she passed Katerina her sparkling gold gown with the little matching jacket.

Kat sidled up to me, her gold gown in her arms. "Please," she whispered. "You must help me not to be seen by Amanda when I am changing my clothes."

"No problem," I said. "Just stick near me." I turned to Cassandra. "Hey, Cass," I whispered, "create a diversion, okay?"

"You got it," said Cassandra with a wink.

She walked over to Amanda, her gown in her arms.

"Amanda," she said. "I think this dress is damaged."

"You're kidding," Amanda said. She sighed. "Where? Let's see."

That was my cue. I hurried Katerina over to the far corner of the dressing room and stood in front of her.

"Go," I hissed over my shoulder. "Now."

I could hear Katerina whimpering a little as she changed into her gown. Cassandra was talking a blue streak on the other side of the room.

"Now, I know I saw a rip here somewhere," she was saying. She searched through the yards of white fabric that made up the full skirt of her gown. "Where *was* it?"

"Well, if you're having that much trouble locating it, it couldn't have been too big," said Amanda as they peered at the gown together.

"Oh, no, I think it was a pretty good size," said Cassandra. She kept pawing through the fabric of her gown.

"Cassandra, wherever it is, it really doesn't seem like something that the camera's going to pick up," said Amanda impatiently. "Why don't you just put the dress on."

"All right," whispered Katerina over my shoulder. "I have finished."

Cassandra glanced toward the corner, and I gave her the thumbs-up sign.

Cassandra gave a dramatic sigh. "Okay," she said to Amanda. "I guess you're right."

She gave Katerina and me another quick wink as she started changing into her gown. When we were finished dressing, we joined Pia, Naira, and Paige at poolside. It had seemed like a strange idea to shoot evening gowns at a pool, but now that we were out there I could see that the pool area was the perfect setting.

The pool was perfectly round, with a small

sparkling fountain illuminated by a pale pink light in its center. Surrounding the pool and stretching up toward the glass ceiling were thick white columns with vines wrapped around them.

"Oh, good, everyone's ready," said Leslie when she saw us. She turned to Jackie. "This is what I was thinking. We've got all these columns here. What if we started by standing the models between the columns, perfectly straight, arms at their sides, very simple? Almost as if they were columns themselves come to life."

"Very nice," said Jackie. "With complicated clothes like these, a simple pose would be very dramatic."

"Okay, girls," said Leslie, "this is where I want you...." She directed us each to a spot between two columns. "Now, face front and stand as straight as possible," she said.

It was an interesting pose. Standing there like that made me feel like I was in the army or something. Standing so still also made me feel really sleepy. I wished I had been able to sleep a little more the night before.

"Relax, girls," Jackie directed. "It's a simple pose, but it doesn't have to be stiff."

I took a deep breath in and let it out. As I did, I felt my body relax.

"Better," said Jackie. Then she looked in my direction and frowned. "Natalie, is there something strange going on with Kerri's makeup? She doesn't look quite right."

"Well, I had to use a little extra cover stick on her today," she said.

Jackie walked over to me and peered at me.

"Kerri, dear, what's going on?" she said, frowning again. "You don't look yourself."

"I'm kind of tired," I admitted. "Maybe I didn't get enough sleep last night."

"I would say not." Jackie shook her head. "Natalie, is this the best we can do with her?"

"Yes, I'm afraid so," Natalie answered.

I couldn't help feeling bad. I knew I didn't look my best.

Jackie looked around. "Katerina," she called, "relax, dear. Try to loosen up a little."

I glanced at Katerina out of the corner of my eye. She looked like a mannequin in a store window, holding herself rigid to keep the scratchy fabric of her gown from rubbing against her tender back.

Leslie shot a few and then looked up from

her camera and frowned. "She's still looking too stiff."

"Katerina," Jackie said again, "loosen up a little. Your shoulders are really tight."

Katerina shifted a bit. Her mouth was pinched and I could see her trying to hold back a wince.

"Here," said Jackie, walking toward her. "I know what to do." She walked behind Katerina and reached out for her shoulders. "A quick massage will loosen you right up."

Jackie's hands touched her shoulders. Katerina let out a howl that echoed through the pool area.

"I don't know what you three girls were thinking," Jackie said later in her hotel suite.

I hung my head. "We're sorry," I said.

Cassandra shifted uneasily beside me. "We were wrong not to tell you," she said.

"It is my fault," Katerina said tearfully. "Kerri and Cassandra were only trying to help me."

"Well," said Jackie, "if they had truly had your best interests at heart, they would have come to me immediately. A bad burn like that can be dangerous, you know. You're lucky it didn't put you in the hospital."

Katerina nodded, stifling a sob.

Jackie sat down on the couch with a sigh.

"Look," she said, "I like you girls, I really do. But you have to realize that you're professionals now. You came down here to do a job, and you have certain responsibilities. Not just to me, and not just to the Fords, but to yourselves."

I nodded. I knew she was right.

"That means taking care of yourselves in every way you can," Jackie went on. "Eating right, protecting your skin"—she looked at me—"and getting enough sleep, too."

She sighed. "Well, that's it, girls, no more lecture," she said. "You can go now."

The three of us walked down the hall to our room. Inside, Katerina sat down gingerly in a chair, and Cassandra and I flopped on our beds.

"I am very sorry for the trouble I have caused you both," said Katerina. "I know now that this was wrong to ask you to—how do you say it—cover up like that."

"That's okay, Kat," I said.

"Yeah," said Cassandra. "Just make sure

146

that next time you go to the beach you do some covering up of your own."

I smiled at Cassandra's joke, but inside I felt terrible. The past few days had just seemed like such a mess. I'd been looking forward to this trip so much, but nothing had gone right. Seeing Heather and Jessa hadn't turned out the way I'd imagined. And now Jackie was upset with me, too. It was just amazing how out of place I felt in my own hometown.

Then, I had a thought. I had the rest of the day free, and I knew where I wanted to spend it.

I picked up the phone and dialed.

"Hi, Mom!" I said. "It's me, Kerri."

CHAPTER 13

"Wow, look at this one," said my sister Casey. She picked up a loose photograph from the cardboard box on the floor in front of us. She passed it to my sister Andie.

"Aw, how cute," said Andie. "Look at Kerri."

I took the picture from her. It showed the three of us, all dressed up for Easter. Five-year-old Andie was wearing a cute little yellow plaid dress with puffy sleeves. Casey was three and was wearing the same dress, in pink. And there I was, as a two-year-old, dressed in nothing but my diaper.

"Oh, I remember that day," sighed my mother, looking over my shoulder. "Grandma Belle had made those three adorable little dresses. We were all going over there for Easter dinner, so I wanted you all to wear them.

148

But Kerri absolutely refused to put hers on." She laughed. "I ended up taking you over in a pair of overalls."

I laughed, too. "I guess even back then I wasn't really into dressing up," I said.

It was late afternoon. The four of us had finished the huge lunch my mom had made, and for the past hour or so we'd been looking through boxes of old family photographs. It felt great to just be hanging around with my mom and sisters. I was more relaxed and happy than I'd been since I had arrived in Florida.

Andie picked up another photo. "Oh, and here we are at Christmas," she said. "Gosh, remember how we used to spray the windows white to look like snow?"

"You know, it took me forever to figure out that that was why we were doing it," I said, taking the picture from her. I laughed. "For years I thought that spraying your windows white was just some kind of Christmas tradition that everybody did. You know, like decorating a tree or something."

"It's pretty ridiculous, if you think about it," said Casey. "I mean, trying to make it look like there's snow on the windows when it's eighty degrees outside."

"Well, as I remember, you enjoyed it very much at the time, my dear," said my mother. "In fact, you were the one who always asked to do the spraying. Who knows? Maybe that was even one of the reasons you ended up being so artistic."

"Mom," Casey moaned, "spraying fake snow on the windows is not artistic."

"Hey, Mom," I said, pulling out a small, battered-looking photo. "Who's this in the picture with you?"

The photograph showed a very young version of my mother, with long, straight, blond hair. She was dressed in a pair of striped bell-bottom pants and a turtleneck, and she was leaning against the hood of a car. Next to her was another girl, with long, wavy, dark hair parted in the middle, wearing a peasant blouse and a miniskirt. They had their arms around each other's shoulders.

She took the picture from me.

"Oh, that's Cathy Travis," she said.

"Who?" asked Casey.

"Cathy Travis," said my mother. "From when I lived in Maryland. She was my absolute best friend in the world, at the time."

"What happened to her?" I asked.

"Nothing happened to her," said my mother. "We just sort of drifted apart." She sighed. "I married your father. Then we moved down here, so Cathy and I didn't really see each other anymore. I still get a card from her now and then, though."

"Gosh," said Casey. "And she used to be your best friend. How sad."

"Not really," said my mother, putting down the photo. "As time went on, we just had less and less in common. We didn't feel quite as close as we once were, that's all. Sometimes that happens with old friends. If you're lucky, you're always making new friends along the way as well."

"Yeah," I said, thinking. Maybe that was what was happening to me a little right now. Maybe it was natural to feel a little less close to Heather and Jessa than I used to since I'd moved away and was making new friends.

I thought of Cassandra, of how close we'd started to get over the past couple of months, and of my other housemates. The more time we spent together living, working, and just going through things, the better we understood one another. Which was pretty cool, considering that we all came from different backgrounds. After this trip, even Katerina, who I had once thought was so cold and distant, seemed like a friend.

Casey sat back and stretched. "Okay, I've had about enough of these old pictures," she said. "What do you say we go to the movies? The new Devon Redmond movie is playing at the mall."

"Devon Redmond's in South Beach right now, you know," I said. I looked at my watch. "And at this very moment he's talking to my friend Cassandra."

"Wow," said Andie. "Really?"

I nodded. "She's doing an interview with him for a TV show in Brazil," I said.

"Isn't that marvelous," said my mother. "She must be thrilled."

"Yeah, I guess," I said. Cassandra was definitely excited about doing the interview. But I knew she was still a little disappointed that she wouldn't be able to appear on camera with Devon Redmond.

"Gee, now the idea of seeing him on a movie screen doesn't sound quite as exciting to me," joked Casey.

"No, let's go," said Andie. "It'll be fun."

"I'm in," I said. "Mom?"

"No thanks, honey," she said. "You girls go ahead. I have some things I want to get done around the house."

"Okay, Mom," I said, standing up. "Oh, and Mom?"

"Yes, dear, what is it?" she asked.

"Thanks," I said. "This was the best."

"So, how did your friend Cassandra manage to get this interview with Devon Redmond?" asked Casey, as the three of us stood in line at the mall to buy our movie tickets.

"Cass is totally the best at stuff like that," I said. "When she really wants something, she almost always manages to get it."

"Well, I guess that's a useful skill," said Andie.

"Yeah," I said. "Like this one time, when she was up for this big job for a Janelle jeans campaign. They were looking for someone who was a little wild, so she did all these nutty things at the go-see like jumping on the furniture and stuff."

"Was that the ad with the guy and the girl on the roller coaster?" asked Casey.

I nodded. "That was Cass. The funny thing

is, she's really scared of roller coasters. But she went on it anyway, because she really wanted to do the ad."

"She does sound determined," said Andie.

"Yeah," I said. "The interview thing started when she met Devon Redmond in the elevator at our hotel. She got in and started talking to him about the way it looked. The next thing she knew, he was giving her an architecture lesson and agreeing to do an interview with her." I shook my head. "She's incredible."

We arrived at the box office and bought our tickets.

"Should we get some popcorn?" asked Andie.

"I'll get it," I said. "You guys go save us some good seats."

Andie and Casey headed into the theater, and I went over to the concession stand. I got a big bucket of popcorn for us to share. As I turned to head into the theater, I suddenly heard a familiar voice.

"Kerri!"

I turned and saw Heather and Jessa. Heather was holding a bucket of popcorn and Jessa had a candy bar and a soda.

"Oh, hi," I said.

"Hi, Kerri," said Heather.

"What are you doing here?" asked Jessa.

"Um, going to the movies," I said.

"Oh," said Heather. She had a funny expression on her face. "Who are you here with?"

"I'm with Casey and Andie," I said. "I just ate lunch at my mom's."

"Why didn't you tell us you were going to be in Laurel Beach?" asked Jessa.

"I don't get it," said Heather. "We could have gotten together."

"I didn't know I was going to be here until today," I said. "I just decided to call up my mom and my sisters and stop by."

"Well, you could have called us, too," Jessa pointed out. "I mean, if you wanted to get together, that is."

"Come on, you guys," I said, feeling a little hurt. "You know that's not it."

"Are you sure, Kerri?" asked Jessa. Her lip was trembling.

"Jess, come on," I said again.

"We have hardly seen you at all since you got here, Kerri," Heather pointed out.

"But there was nothing I could do about that," I said. I was getting more and more upset. "I wanted to spend time with you guys, but my schedule's been really, really busy. You don't understand what it's like." As I spoke I could feel a lump forming in my throat. "And today I just wanted to see my mom and my sisters for a little while before my plane leaves at seven o'clock tomorrow morning," I said.

"Fine," said Jessa. "You don't have to explain it to us. You can spend time with anyone you want." She turned to Heather. "Come on, Heath, let's get going. We don't want to miss the movie."

She took Heather by the arm and they turned away. As they did, I got a terrible feeling in my stomach. I hate it when people get upset with me. And that it was Jessa and Heather who were mad at me made me feel even worse than usual. I just stood beside the concession stand for a while trying not to cry.

I thought back to how close the three of us had been before I had moved to New York. I understood that maybe we couldn't be quite like that now, and that maybe Jessa and Heather had grown a little closer since I had moved away. But we were all still friends, weren't we? Why was it that nothing at all had seemed to go right between me and my Laurel Beach friends on this trip?

I turned to walk into the darkened theater, where my sisters were waiting. But I had no desire to see the movie at all anymore. I looked down at the bucket of popcorn in my hands and hoped Andie and Casey were hungry, because I'd completely lost my appetite.

CHAPTER 14

The next morning my housemates and I stood in line at the security checkpoint in the Miami airport with the people from *Style*.

"Well, girls," said Jackie, "I would say that all-in-all it was a very successful trip. We had a few little mishaps"—she glanced at Katerina, who was still standing a little stiffly—"but nothing major. And I think Leslie got some very good shots." She turned to Alex, who was next to her. "You've got all the tickets?"

He patted the pocket of his blazer. "Right here," he answered.

"I can't believe we're leaving this sunny weather and going back to New York," said Amanda with a sigh. "I'm really going to miss it."

"Me, too," said Paige. "But I miss Jordan more."

"*Alora*, well, I will miss very much the wonderful shopping," said Pia. She held up a large shoulder bag. "I needed another entire bag to carry all of my purchases home with. *Fortunatamente*, luckily, Naira came to rescue me with this one. *Mille grazie*. A million thank-yous."

"No problem. I always pack an extra bag just in case," said Naira.

As the line moved forward into the "Passengers Only" section, Cassandra turned to me.

"Are you okay?" she asked me quietly. "You don't seem like yourself."

"I don't know," I said. "I guess this trip didn't go exactly the way I thought it would."

"But you really did great work," she said. "I know, you had that little problem with being tired at the Palm Club shoot, but other than that—"

"No, no, it's not that," I said. "Modeling was fine."

"What was it, then?" she said. "Did something happen with your family?"

I shook my head. "My family was great. I got to see my mom and my dad. And when I talked to my dad yesterday, he said he would be up in New York on business soon." I paused. "No, the problem was with my friends." I looked at her. "My old friends, that is. I don't know. We just didn't seem to get along the way we used to."

"That's too bad," said Cassandra.

"Yeah," I said sadly. "It sure is."

Just then, I heard familiar voices calling my name.

"Kerri! Kerri!"

I turned in disbelief, thinking I must be hearing things. But there, running toward the security checkpoint, laughing and panting, were Heather and Jessa.

"Oh my gosh," I said to Cassandra. "I can't believe it. There they are."

They came through the metal detector, waving and calling to me.

"Go ahead," said Cassandra. "You've still got about a minute before we board."

"Okay," I said. "Hold my place. I'll be right back."

I hurried toward them.

"You guys!" I said. "I can't believe this! What are you doing here?"

Heather glanced at Jessa.

"We came to see you off, Kerri," she said.

"Yeah," said Jessa. She looked at me. "We didn't want to leave with things the way they were. I'm really sorry about what happened at the movies yesterday."

"Same here," I said, feeling that lump creep back into my throat. "I hated to think I was leaving with you guys mad at me like that."

"We *were* kind of hard on you," said Heather. "It was just that we were hurt that you didn't call us."

"You know, we just thought it was going to be like old times," said Jessa.

"Me, too," I said. "And I'm sorry. I wanted to see you guys. It was just that—"

Jessa stopped me. "You don't have to explain to us." She smiled. "And this time, I mean it."

"Besides, we should have realized it could never be exactly like old times," said Heather.

I looked at them and felt tears spring into my eyes. "You guys are the best," I said. "I can't believe you got up this early and came out here like this before school."

"We had to," said Heather. She handed me a large plastic bag. "We didn't want you to leave without these."

I took the bag. "What is this?" I asked.

"See for yourself," Jessa said with a giggle.

I looked in and recognized the pile of green and white inside it right away. "Oh wow," I said. I blinked back my tears. "Laurel Lions pom-poms! I can't believe it."

"We know you returned yours at the end of the season last year like you were supposed to," said Jessa. "But we figured it wouldn't hurt to bend the rules a little and let you have some."

"Yeah," said Heather. She grinned. "Once a Laurel Lions cheerleader, always a Laurel Lions cheerleader, right?"

"Right," I said, smiling.

Just then, I heard Cassandra calling me.

"Kerri, come on! We're boarding!"

"I'd better get going or I'm going to miss my plane," I said. We all hugged each other. "It was great to see you guys. Next time I'll come for a *real* visit."

"You'd better," said Heather. "But seriously, it really was great to see you."

"Yeah," said Jessa. She grinned. "Now don't go and turn into a Northerner on us, Kerr."

I hugged the bag of pom-poms to my chest.

"Don't worry," I said. I could feel my eyes fill with tears, but this time it was because I was happy. "I won't."

"Kerri! Come on!" called Cassandra again. I looked and saw that she and Alex were the only two who hadn't boarded the plane. Alex looked very agitated, and he was beckoning to me wildly.

"Okay, here I come!" I called. I turned back to Heather and Jessa. "Bye, you guys! I'll call you soon!"

"Bye!" they called.

I ran to where Cassandra and Alex were waiting, my heart pounding. Alex handed me my ticket, and the flight attendants hurried us onto the plane moments before the doors were shut.

"*Puxa*, wow!" said Cassandra, falling into the seat next to mine. "Talk about living dangerously. I thought we were going to miss it." She grinned. "Or that Alex was going to have a heart attack."

I stood up to stuff the bag with the pompoms in the storage space above the seat. Cassandra handed me the shoulder bag that held her video camera to put up as well.

"Hey, Cass," I said, "you haven't told me how the interview with Devon Redmond went yesterday."

She grinned at me. "Great," she said. "I think Roberto's going to be impressed when he sees the chemistry between me and Devon."

"What do you mean?" I asked, as the plane's engines started. "How can he tell? Devon's the only one on camera. You were doing the taping, right?"

"Well, yes and no," she said, looking at me slyly. "Or rather, no and yes."

"Cass," I said, "what *are* you talking about?"

"No, Devon's not the only one on camera, but yes, I was doing the taping," she said.

"Huh?" I said. "How is that possible?"

"Not only was it possible," said Cassandra, as the plane started down the runway, "but it was unavoidable. You see, one of the places Devon took me on that architecture tour was this great old hotel called the Carlson." She raised one eyebrow. "And the Carlson is famous for its mirrored lobby."

"So you happened to decide to tape the interview there!" I finished.

"Well, naturally I had to tape Devon in one of the architectural landmarks he's working so hard to preserve," she said coyly.

"Natch," I agreed, laughing.

I shook my head. Sometimes I thought Cass was the most amazing person I had ever met. I didn't know anyone else who was like her in the least.

The plane lifted off the ground. I turned to look out the window. Below us was the ocean, looking like a big blue sheet.

I turned to Cassandra.

"Hey," I said, "let's go to the Cocoa Bean when we get back."

"Okay," she said. "You got it." She looked at me. "But only if we can get a table by the window."

book (or **portfolio**): a collection of a model's current photos and tear sheets. Clients look at these books to choose the models they want to hire. A model's book can make or break her career.

booker (or **agent**): the person responsible for a model's day-to-day schedule. Bookers may speak to their models as often as ten times a day!

booking: a scheduled modeling job.

client: a company, magazine, or photographer who hires a model.

comp (or **comp card**): short for "composite." A comp is like an oversized postcard with a model's photos on it. Usually there is a big photo on the front of the comp and two or three smaller photos on the back. A comp includes the name of the model and her agency. Agencies send comps out to prospective clients for reference. Models use comps like business cards.

fitting: a special appointment for models to try on the clothes that they'll be wearing. Fittings are scheduled so that clothes can be altered to fit the model or models who will be wearing them in the shoot. It's also a chance to see what pieces of clothing go best together, and which models look best in which outfits.

location vans: big trailers or mobile homes that are set up at an outdoor shoot location. Location vans are used as makeup rooms, dressing rooms, and offices by the models and the people running the shoot.

stylist: a person who chooses the clothes and accessories for a shoot.